"Elliott? Ca...

Paul took a deep br... able—impersonate hi... aged to grin.

But his smile faltered when Katherine flung herself into his arms. "Are you really okay? Are you really *real?*"

Before he could answer, she ran her hand over his hair. "Your hair's shorter," she murmured, her words sounding shaky with disbelief. "The mustache is gone and your clothes…"

Paul blinked. Details he hadn't thought of. Details that hadn't seemed important in the face of Matthew's disappearance. "They wanted to clean me up at the hospital."

She made a choking sound, one that wavered between a sob and a laugh, the laughter dominating. "You must be tired. Here I am rambling on when you need to get to bed."

Paul's head jerked upward suddenly. Another detail he hadn't thought of.

Katherine put her arm around his waist. Brows rising, her unusual eyes darkened to a shade somewhere between coy and alluring. "You deserve a proper welcome home. I want you to know just how much you were missed."

Belatedly it occurred to him that this was no minor detail.

Dear Reader,

Each story is inspired by such very different events, feelings…sometimes just a whisper of an idea. I have always been fascinated by twins, the bond they share—in fact, the special bond felt by all siblings (especially since I have the world's best big brother).

I marvel at the possibility of looking at another human being and seeing your own face. As an identical twin, your thoughts and feelings are linked to those of another person—it must be incredible. And what if you're not a twin but a woman who falls in love with a twin…and his brother?

Please join me on Katherine Crowden's adventure, one that also explores the issues of friendship and blended families.

I would love to hear from you. Please write c/o Harlequin Superromance, 225 Duncan Mill Road, Don Mills, ON, M3B 3K9 Canada.

Sincerely,

Bonnie K. Winn

THE WRONG BROTHER
Bonnie K. Winn

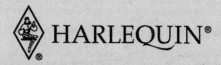

HARLEQUIN®

TORONTO • NEW YORK • LONDON
AMSTERDAM • PARIS • SYDNEY • HAMBURG
STOCKHOLM • ATHENS • TOKYO • MILAN • MADRID
PRAGUE • WARSAW • BUDAPEST • AUCKLAND

ISBN 0-373-70898-X

THE WRONG BROTHER

Copyright © 2000 by Bonnie K. Winn.

All rights reserved. Except for use in any review, the reproduction or utilization of this work in whole or in part in any form by any electronic, mechanical or other means, now known or hereafter invented, including xerography, photocopying and recording, or in any information storage or retrieval system, is forbidden without the written permission of the publisher, Harlequin Enterprises Limited, 225 Duncan Mill Road, Don Mills, Ontario, Canada M3B 3K9.

All characters in this book have no existence outside the imagination of the author and have no relation whatsoever to anyone bearing the same name or names. They are not even distantly inspired by any individual known or unknown to the author, and all incidents are pure invention.

This edition published by arrangement with Harlequin Books S.A.

® and TM are trademarks of the publisher. Trademarks indicated with ® are registered in the United States Patent and Trademark Office, the Canadian Trade Marks Office and in other countries.

Visit us at www.romance.net

Printed in U.S.A.

Special thanks to Jean Baker, Becky Burton and Mary Jo Westien for your invaluable assistance and expertise.

And to Paula Eykelhof for your belief.

DEDICATION

In memory of Brian Paul Case. You left us too soon, but you'll never be forgotten.
October 2, 1977 – May 5, 1999

PROLOGUE

Chicago

THE PAIN WAS SHARP, almost unbearable in its intensity. Paul Elliott sucked in his breath. The last time he'd come anywhere near this sort of feeling, his twin brother, Matthew, had fractured his back in a skiing accident. Once, they'd been close enough to read each other's thoughts, feel each other's pain.

Again Paul regretted the last-minute changes in his work schedule that had forced him to cancel his meeting with Matthew. Although they had been estranged longer than he wanted to admit, Paul had been looking forward to the trip. He'd missed his twin, the unique bond they'd shared as brothers and friends. It was time to renew their relationship, to try to put the past where it belonged, to heal the painful rift that had torn them apart.

Matthew had called to say their Piper Saratoga was in tip-top shape and then had hesitantly asked Paul to visit and meet his bride. Previously Matthew had tried to repair their break, but Paul had refused. Taking the step into marriage seemed to unleash a new determination in his twin—Matthew had again

felt the need to embrace family. The irony of the
reason for the contact wasn't lost on Paul, but he
also knew that eventually he had to accept Matthew's overtures.

Not only did it seem forever since they'd seen
each other, it also seemed forever since they'd taken
to the sky to test their wings. Despite their estrangement, the brothers continued to share ownership of
the Piper PA 32, a sweet plane that neither had been
willing to relinquish. Although Paul wasn't one to
credit symbolism, in many ways the plane was the
sole thread that kept their relationship from complete dissolution. Because they both owned the
plane, they couldn't walk away from each other permanently.

And although it had remained unsaid, it was time
to reestablish the twin bond that had kept them close
since birth. Close, that is, until that one seemingly
irreparable break.

Frowning, Paul wished they hadn't also argued
about money. They'd had enough damage to repair
already. But his brother had never really had a head
for finances, and certainly even less since his recent
marriage. Matthew had bragged about his new bride,
but privately Paul was concerned about the amount
of money Matthew had spent since his elopement.
The bills had flowed into their shared trust with
alarming speed and frequency. The latest purchase
was a Porsche.

Paul couldn't help wondering if Katherine was a

greedy seductress who thought she'd hit the jackpot. Could that be why Matthew had continued to need so much money, to the point of asking for yet another loan from their shared interests?

Paul knew he would have to reschedule the visit since Matthew was eager for him to meet his new wife. Their conversation had been awkward, stilted. It had been too long since they'd shared a simple laugh. It had been too long for many things.

However, during their brief conversation, Matthew had told him that Katherine didn't know they were twins, didn't even know they were brothers. Matthew had confessed he hadn't wanted to admit the extent of their estrangement or his own culpability.

It occurred to Paul that there was much Matthew hadn't told him about Katherine, and clearly there was much his brother hadn't revealed to her, either. Fun-loving Matthew had a bit of a Peter Pan complex, one that tended to make him put off dealing with unpleasantness. Paul just hoped it hadn't led him to trouble.

The pain struck again, sharp and swift. In its wake he felt an amazing sense of loss, a bereft feeling he'd never before experienced. As he steeled himself against the double onslaught of feelings, his cell phone rang. Foreboding arrived at precisely the same instant.

Cautiously Paul picked up the phone. "Elliott."

He listened, his brain accepting what his gut had already acknowledged.

"I'll be on the next plane."

South Carolina Coast

THE GRAVEYARD of the Atlantic. Aptly named, the diamond shoals of the South Carolina coast were the wicked wonder of the Eastern seaboard. Gulf currents and southbound Labrador currents collided there, making the area one of the most dangerous places in the Atlantic.

And that was where Matthew's plane had gone down, not far from where he lived.

A full-scale rescue operation began immediately. Especially when Paul pressed every contact he possessed into service. And as a CIA agent, he had a considerable number of contacts. The Coast Guard had pulled out all the stops for the search-and-rescue mission. Numerous rescue ships and divers were combing the area, putting all available high-tech equipment to efficient use.

The Barrier islands of the outer banks were beautiful but treacherous. Underwater ledges and coves provided innumerable places to catch and trap a body.

Paul couldn't bring himself to think of Matthew as a body yet. Officially his brother was listed as missing. Remembering all the scrapes the two of them had survived, Paul couldn't believe Matthew wouldn't survive this one, too. Besides, his twin had always possessed a mercurial quality, able to glide blithely over trouble and come out unscathed. Paul expected to see his brother's grinning face any moment. Full of jokes, Matthew would needle him for even worrying.

And right now Paul would give his own arms and legs to see that teasing face, that unquenchable grin. Grimly he looked out over the endless miles of water. If he didn't see Matthew alive again, he would know why. And he would start with his brother's gold-digging bride.

CHAPTER ONE

KATHERINE PACED the length of the kitchen, her gaze going again to the view of the ocean, visible through the tall wide windows. She returned again and again to this room, the warm center of the house that Elliott had kept alive with his laughter.

She only prayed his incredible spirit had kept him alive, as well. Her ribs ached from the sobs that had racked her body when the search had turned up nothing. Until that moment she was certain he would arrive home with his crooked grin and a wildly exaggerated tale of the crash and his success at cheating death.

But three days had now passed. Although the search was continuing, hope had dimmed with each passing hour, each effort that produced nothing. The divers had surfaced with a seemingly endless collection of tires, seaweed, timbers and other trash. But no sign of her husband.

"Katherine, how about some tea?" her friend Jessica asked, crossing to the stove where the kettle had been whistling for the past few minutes.

Katherine didn't take her gaze from the window

as she replied distractedly, "Hmm? Tea? No thanks."

Jessica didn't remind Katherine that she had put the kettle on herself, thinking some tea would be soothing. It was clear Katherine's mind was elsewhere, as it had been ever since they'd heard the dreadful news.

Jessica prepared the tea and added a dollop of honey to the steaming brew. "I think I'll have some, if you don't mind. Why don't you join me?"

The rephrasing seemed to work. "Oh, sure," Katherine murmured, still staring through the windows. "How long do you suppose someone can stay alive in the ocean?"

Out of Katherine's line of vision, Jessica flinched, then closed her eyes briefly. "I suppose it depends. I've heard stories about people who survived for several days hanging on to nothing more than a plank."

"And some people don't last more than a few hours," Katherine replied, the tears seeping into her voice.

"You can't think that way," Jessica cautioned her. "You know what a fighter Matthew is. You can't give up on him."

Katherine reached blindly for her friend's hand. "What would I do without you to see me through this?"

Jessica gave her a reassuring hug. "Let's don't ever find out, okay? You've always been there for me.'' Tactfully Jessica didn't remind Katherine what a great friend she'd been when Jessica had lost her own husband.

Katherine turned again to stare at the ocean. "He loves the water, you know."

"He's smart…resourceful," Jessica tried again, afraid to build up her friend's hopes too much, yet knowing she needed *some* bolstering to keep her from entering an abyss of grief prematurely.

"And that damn plane," Katherine continued as though Jessica hadn't spoken. "He loves that plane. The way he lavished attention on it, you'd have thought the two of *them* were newlyweds."

Jessica winced again. A crisis like this was difficult enough when a couple had years of strength to fall back on. But Elliott and Katherine had only been together a few short months. They were still on their honeymoon.

"You'd think the plane would be in perfect shape with all that attention," Katherine said. A hiccuping sigh punctuated the words, and Jessica suspected tears weren't far behind. Katherine spun away from the window. "Makes you wonder how it could possibly have crashed."

It was an observation Katherine had made more than once since she'd been notified. Why would a plane in perfect mechanical condition crash? Jessica tried to think of some way to divert her friend's attention. "Katherine, maybe we should go out for a walk, get some fresh air. Clear our minds."

"There's not enough fresh air in the world to clear my mind," Katherine replied, pushing back her long curling dark hair. Then she patted her friend's arm. "But I appreciate the thought. Maybe you'd like some air, though. I'll be fine."

Jessica stared helplessly at her friend. It was so like Katherine to think of others, even in a desperate situation like this. "I should go get Brian. My mother's probably had about as much of a five-year-old boy as she can stand. Why don't you come with me? We can stop and have some dinner. My treat."

"I should stay by the phone."

"You can forward it to your cell phone," Jessica reminded her.

Katherine's smile was bleak. "I know. I'd rather stay here, though. It probably sounds silly, but it's as if I need to keep my own vigil."

"A candle burning in the window?" Jessica asked gently.

Katherine nodded. "I haven't really given up on Matthew, you know, no matter what I say." She looked out again toward the ocean. "And if I'm here, then the house won't be empty when…when Matthew strolls up the path."

Jessica's heart ached for her friend. "I could ask my mother to drop Brian off here. We could order pizza—"

"No, you go on. I'm fine. I wouldn't mind some quiet time. I need to sort through my thoughts."

"I hate leaving you alone," Jessica protested.

"I'm not alone." Katherine smiled crookedly as she glanced toward the rear of the house. "You can't stay with me twenty-four hours a day, even though I appreciate it. Please, go on, pick up Brian. Give him a kiss for me."

Jessica battled tears of her own, knowing her friend's pain. She remembered her own intense feelings of loss, how hard it was to climb from that pit of pain. "Tell you what. I'll pick up Brian, then call you before we decide what to do for dinner."

"Okay. Thanks, friend." Katherine hugged her.

Jessica blinked away her terrible memories and embraced her fiercely. "Don't forget—I'm only ten minutes away."

Katherine managed a smile. "What else do you think keeps me sane?"

THE HOUSE STOOD on a knoll that swept upward from the beach. Past the sands, beyond the wild grass. A shell-topped road wound its way to a lush cultivated lawn. Ancient live oak trees dripping moss flanked the house, while a stalwart magnolia dominated the yard, scenting the air as it stood sentry. The house wasn't the sleek contemporary Paul had expected. Rather, a weathered Cape Cod with soft inviting lines. The shadows of approaching twilight reached over the gables, while the last struggling rays of sun reflected off the ocean.

It wasn't a menacing picture. In fact, quite the

opposite—a Norman Rockwell setting that promised serenity. Grimly Paul wondered if that was the plan.

But it wasn't a plan that deterred him. He reached for the door knocker, but before he could lift it, the door was flung open.

"Elliott?" Katherine's voice was part question, part exclamation. "I saw you coming up the path…" She moved forward hesitantly, her face crumpling. Eyes, apparently swollen from weeping, widened in seeming disbelief as new tears swam in their depths. "Can it really be you?"

Paul took a deep breath, prepared to do the unthinkable. "It's me." Then he managed a grin.

But his smile faltered when Katherine flung herself into his arms. Then her hands were running over his shoulders, down his arms, reaching for his chest. As she did, her body trembled. It was as though she checked both for injuries and to make sure she wasn't imagining him.

"Are you really okay?" Her voice caught. "Are you really *real?* I've been hoping so hard you'd come back that I'm afraid I've conjured you up. I want so much to believe you're here but…I'm afraid I'm dreaming. I've prayed, I've hoped…"

Paul felt her shudder and stepped further into his role, forcing himself to ignore the misgivings her seemingly genuine distress was causing. "I'm real."

Katherine buried her face against his chest. "I was so afraid you weren't coming back. I know you always come out on top, but this time..." She held him even closer. "I can't believe how lucky I am."

Paul mimicked his brother's style. "Hey, babe, I'm a survivor."

Slowly Katherine pulled back. Again he forced himself to stand still as she ran her hand over his hair, then gently cupped his jaw. "Your hair's shorter," she murmured, her words coated, it seemed, with shaky disbelief. "The mustache is gone, and your clothes..."

Paul blinked. Details he hadn't thought of. Details that hadn't seemed important in the face of Matthew's disappearance...possibly his death. He swallowed the sharp pain of that last thought, forcing himself to adopt his brother's more casual demeanor. "They wanted to clean me up in the hospital."

"Hospital?" she asked. Paul wondered if the fear threaded through her voice could be real. It quivered as she clutched his arms, her face registering worry.

"Sure." He forced another grin, knowing Matthew would be wearing one, praying that somewhere he still was. "They don't just pull you out of the water and send you straight home. I had a concussion. Didn't the nurse who phoned tell you?"

"No one called," she replied, her hands stroking him tentatively, before again burying her head against his chest. "I was by the phone day and night, hoping to hear from you—or about you."

Paul purposely hadn't let one of the operatives

phone with the news he had been "found." He wanted to view firsthand the expression on her face, her reaction when she saw him. Remembering Matthew's easygoing body language, he made his shrug deliberately casual. "Someone was supposed to call you."

"It doesn't matter," she murmured, as her gaze continued skimming over him. "Nothing else matters except that you're safe. I kept thinking that you might not be coming home. Every day—every hour—was agony. I kept picturing so many horrible things without you here to tell me to be brave...to always think positively. I tried, I really did, but I knew we needed a miracle for you to survive." Her voice sounded choked with feeling. "And we got the miracle."

He squirmed beneath Katherine's intense words. If her act was genuine, his behavior was unbearably callous. "I'm sorry you were so worried."

"Worried?" she cried. "Oh, God. I never knew before how little that word conveys. Not when it means your whole life can change. Or end. Each second that passes is an eternity. But I'd go through it again in an instant, knowing you're safe."

Once again Paul was nonplussed at her admission. He needed to learn the truth, but he didn't want to hurt this woman if she wasn't involved in sabotaging Matthew's plane.

"How long were you in the hospital?" she asked. "Or were you in the water for a long time?"

"I'm not really sure," Paul improvised. He couldn't tell her that he hadn't been able to give up on Matthew, that even though it wasn't possible, he had wanted to personally search every inch of the crash site. "With the disorientation from the head injury it took me a while to get help."

Katherine lifted a hand to touch his head again, then stilled the movement as though afraid to hurt him. Then, if possible, even more concern suffused her face. "Head injury? You said a concussion, didn't you? How bad?"

"Just enough to put me out for a few days," Paul replied, hoping the explanation would satisfy her. "At least that's what the hospital told me."

He wondered at the loving touch when she began to stroke his cheek. Again she seemed to be seeking reassurance that he had returned. "You're certain there's nothing else, something you're not telling me? You're not just trying to be brave?"

"I'm no hero," Paul replied, surprised by her reaction, the trembling of her slight body, the dazzled shock in her wide eyes, the remnants of tears that had splashed her ivory cheeks. His conscience shifted into overdrive. If he was wrong about her...

"You're *my* hero," she responded softly. Her eyelids flickered shut briefly. "My prayers have been answered. God watched out for you and gave us a miracle. You're home. You're really home." Her eyes opened and she gazed at him. "I don't know why we're so blessed. When I think of Jessica's husband..." The words sputtered out into a muffled sob. "I don't know why some are spared when others aren't, but I'm so grateful. So very grateful."

Paul stared down at this stranger's face. Could she be sincere? Or was she an accomplished actress who had plotted to kill her husband for money? One who even now wondered how he could be alive?

As a CIA agent, however, Paul had learned some acting skills of his own. Deliberately he made his grin a crooked replica of his brother's. "You're right. I am lucky." Ignoring the irony in his words, he pulled her close so that she couldn't read the grim message in his eyes or the anguish that lurked there. "And now that I'm home I'll do the worrying."

"What's there to worry about now? You're safe, you're home, you're alive. That's all that's important. I've worried and cried enough for the next decade." She pulled back slightly and Paul could see her eyes shimmering beneath the last brilliant rays of the sinking sun.

A golden glow from that radiant light seemed to envelop them, illuminating her unusual violet eyes, making them resemble uncut amethysts. For a moment Paul's determination wavered. Was that genuine love he glimpsed in those eyes? Was the relief in her voice true?

"It was worth every moment of anguish, every tear, every prayer," she continued. Again she touched him almost reverently. "I didn't want to give up hope—" her voice broke "—but I almost did. It seemed impossible that you could still be alive.'' More tears burst free, fat drops that rolled down her cheeks unchecked.

Paul struggled with the emotions that clawed at him. Was he being impossibly cruel? Unable to stop the motion, he gently wiped the tears away. Then he tucked a wayward strand of silky black hair behind her ear.

She made a choking sound, one that wavered between a sob and a laugh, the laughter dominating. ''You never could stand the serious stuff.''

He blinked, filled again with suspicion. Her mood had shifted quickly. Too quickly for him to believe her sincerity.

''You must be tired!'' she cried suddenly. ''Here I am rambling on and we need to get you to bed.''

Paul's head jerked up. Another detail he hadn't thought of.

Katherine slipped her arm around his waist as she tilted her face toward his. Her brows rose and her unusual eyes darkened to a shade somewhere between coy and alluring. ''You deserve a proper welcome. I want you to know just how much you were missed.'' Her full lips quivered again, then curved in a smile. ''How very very much you were missed.''

Belatedly it occurred to him that this was no minor detail.

CHAPTER TWO

"I'M NOT ALL THAT TIRED," Paul began as Katherine led him inside. He was facing a line that, while not anticipated, certainly couldn't be crossed.

"You need your rest—no dancing on the tables tonight," she chided him gently as they passed a room that appeared to be a study. She steered him, instead, into an inviting family room with a soaring beamed ceiling, a rock fireplace, rows of built-in cherry-wood bookcases and a cozy window seat that looked out on the ocean. "I know you love being the life of the party, but tonight you'll have to settle for being pampered and spoiled beyond your wildest expectations."

"They made me rest plenty in the hospital," Paul explained, wondering why it hadn't occurred to him that impersonating his brother meant sharing a bed with his bride. The shock of Matthew's accident apparently must have stolen his edge.

"You have a concussion," Katherine reminded him. She turned to him suddenly, burrowing close, surprising him again with both her words and actions. "I almost lost you once. I don't want to take any chances."

Paul purposely ignored how soft she felt in his arms. He tried not to be obvious as he pulled back. "I'm safe now."

She took his hand in hers. "Thank God." Her fingers were moving over his left hand when suddenly they stilled. "Your wedding band's gone!"

Paul couldn't prevent a glance at the telling emptiness on his ring finger. "It must have been lost with my other things."

"Other things?"

"My wallet, keys…"

"Oh. No wonder your clothes are different, too."

He shrugged, much as he knew Matthew would have. "I was pretty much at the mercy of the hospital for a new shirt and jeans."

"The other things can be replaced," she murmured, "and you can't, so I'm glad you're the one thing that made it home." She tightened the pressure of her arm around his waist, almost as though she was hanging on for support. "You didn't tell me how you survived the crash."

Luckily Paul had thought that one out before meeting her. "I parachuted out before the crash. Since the plane's in about a thousand pieces, it was hard to find something to hang on to in the water. I wound up washed ashore pretty far down the coast. Like I said, I was disoriented—that's why it took a while to get to a hospital."

She grasped his hands, hers curling naturally within his palms. "It's a miracle you survived." Her voice trembled. "If you hadn't thought to parachute... Oh, Elliott, what would I have done if you hadn't made it?"

Paul stared at her. If this was an act, she was damn good.

"I know I'm being silly," she added, blinking away fresh tears. "I should be celebrating, not weeping. I thought I was cried out by now. Instead, I can't seem to stop." She pressed close. "I'm just so happy you're safe and you're home." She wiped at the tears that escaped her eyes.

"There's no need to cry," he said awkwardly, uncomfortable with her unrestrained display.

"They're tears of joy," she explained with a radiance that shone through the weeping. Then she tilted her face upward to press her tear-wet lips to his. Surprised by the fire in the caress, Paul didn't immediately respond.

"Mommy?" The small voice startled him, upsetting his already tumultuous thoughts.

Mommy? Paul jerked around. *She has a child? Matthew definitely hadn't mentioned this little addition.*

"Dustin!" She hurried toward the little boy, kneeling down when she reached him. "Mommy's sorry she forgot about you, sweetie," Katherine told him as she scooped him up, and rested him on one hip. She brushed at the dark hair on his forehead, smoothing it away, exposing his round chubby face. "Look who's here—Elliott."

It struck him as odd that Matthew's bride didn't prefer a more intimate term. He and Matthew had used their surname since junior high, when few people could tell them apart. It had been easier to go by Elliott, and the moniker had stuck.

The child struggled to get down, and Katherine set him lightly on his feet. Without hesitation Dustin ran to Paul. "Elly-ut?" he asked, holding out his arms.

Taken aback, Paul stood frozen in place as he stared at the toddler.

"Up!" Dustin demanded.

Disarmed, Paul managed to unbend enough to awkwardly lift the toddler. Warm, soft and smelling of talc, Dustin snuggled in his arms. Huge eyes, the same amazing color as his mother's, blinked up at Paul. Pudgy fingers moved to touch his face. "You home now?"

Paul stared down at him. What had this child meant to his brother? Could this be his son? But Matthew had said he and Katherine had only known each other for a few months before their marriage and they'd only been married three months. This little guy was at least three, maybe four years old. Paul cleared his throat. "Yes, I'm home now."

"We going in the plane?" Dustin asked.

Paul felt the hitch in his chest as he thought of the plane's fate—of what he feared was Matthew's fate. And at the same time he wondered what role his brother had played in this child's life. "I don't think so."

Katherine was at his side immediately. "Dustin, Elliott doesn't want to talk about the plane right now. He's got a boo-boo on his head."

Dustin reached for Paul's head. "Boo-boo?"

Katherine linked her hand with her son's and gently untangled his fingers from Paul's hair. "We have to be careful with Elliott for a few days, punkin. He's had a rough time."

"Mommy cried lots when you were losted," Dustin informed him.

Startled, both adults stared at him.

"I didn't think he saw me," Katherine muttered in an aside to Paul. She held out her hands. "Ready for bedtime, sweetie?"

Shaking his head, Dustin clung a moment longer to Paul. The gesture caused an unfamiliar, unsettling, completely unexpected feeling. But then, he'd never had any experience with children. Especially a child who might be the last link he'd have with Matthew.

"I think tonight calls for some cocoa," Katherine told them both.

Denny's mutinous expression faded. "Okay."

Katherine stared for another moment at Paul and Dustin, puzzlement shadowing her eyes. "You look pretty wiped out. Why don't I take Dustin?"

With the ease of familiarity, Katherine shifted the

child into her arms and Paul realized he must have looked as uncomfortable as he felt.

Katherine set Dustin on the floor. "Punkin, why don't you get your Silly Putty and I'll put on the kettle." As the child scampered off to get one of his favorite toys, Katherine turned back to Paul, concern filling her face. "Elliott, I'm serious. Don't be brave for us. I'm worried about how you look—you're so pale. I think the hospital may have released you prematurely." She stepped closer to stroke his jaw. "They say the brain's a funny thing."

"Mine usually is." He tried to quip the way Matthew would have.

"Quite the comedian, aren't you?" She led him to an overstuffed chair. "I want you to plant yourself and grow lots of roots." She pulled up an ottoman to scoot beneath his legs. "I know you like to make a joke out of everything, but…" Her voice began to tremble again. "You don't know what it was like, waiting, wondering…hoping. And now that you're home I can't stand the thought that you might not take care of yourself and you could still…" Her voice trailed off as she bent her head, waves of shiny black hair hiding her face.

This woman was far, far from what Paul had expected. Still, he had to behave like Matthew. "Okay, you win. No more taking chances."

She lifted her head, wiping at errant tears. A ghost of a smile emerged. "Good. This chance was enough to last me until we're ninety, maybe a hundred.''

''Planning that far ahead?''

Her smile grew as she rose. ''Of course. Those vows we took didn't come with an expiration date. You're stuck with me, heartthrob, until you die.''

A chill raced through him at her words.

''Elly-ut!'' The child's cry rang through the air as Dustin ran into the room and launched himself at Paul again.

''Dustin!'' Katherine chided. ''Remember, we have to be careful with Elliott.''

''Careful,'' Dustin agreed, his little head bobbing. Then he pulled a stuffed toy from behind his back. ''For Elly-ut's boo-boo.''

Taken aback, Paul gingerly accepted the teddy bear. ''Don't you like to play with this?'' he asked, awkwardly holding the toy and wondering what to do with it.

''Well, it is his favorite, you know,'' Katherine told him, that same look of puzzlement crossing her face. Then she glanced down at her son. ''Do you think Bobby Bear will help Elliott get better?''

Dustin nodded soberly. ''Bobby will fix him.''

Despite his deception, Paul felt an unexpected warmth as he met Dustin's unblinking gaze. His mother might be a black widow, but the child was an innocent. ''You may be right, Dustin.'' Paul held the bear closer. ''I think I'm already feeling a little better.'' He rubbed the imaginary lump on his head. ''Yep, I'm definitely feeling better.''

Katherine's grin lit her face, transforming it. Up until then all he had seen was concern and relief. The way she looked now was something else. Something unexpectedly appealing.

''My best guys,'' Katherine murmured. Blowing kisses, she backed away, leaving the room.

Dustin continued staring at him.

''So…'' Paul began. What did you say to a kid this size? Paul was vaguely aware of some purple creature that drove parents crazy, and he guessed kids still liked cartoons. But what cartoons were popular now? It occurred to Paul he knew more about genetic research than he did about what interested children. And that wasn't much.

''Bobby Bear wanted you to come home,'' Dustin announced.

Paul cleared his throat, knowing he was on unsteady ground. ''I'm glad, 'cause I wanted to come home, too.''

''You won't go away anymore?'' Dustin asked, his brows pulled together in concentration.

Very unsteady ground. ''Why would I want to do that?''

''My daddy did. Before I was borned.''

A little piece of Paul's heart fractured. Jeez, why did people do stuff like that to little kids, anyway? ''Well, that was him, not me.''

Dustin snuggled closer for a moment, then he pulled back. "Play trains?"

"I don't see why not. We—"

"None of that," Katherine interrupted, returning to the room with a tray. "Dustin, Elliott can't play trains until we're sure he's all better. I imagine the doctor will want to give him a checkup tomorrow or the next day and then we'll see, okay?"

The doctor? Damn. He would have to get a physician secured through the agency.

"The water was already hot," Katherine explained. "I'd just had some tea. So the cocoa's all ready. Dustin, go hop on your mat."

Dustin obliged without complaint, waiting while Katherine handed him his special cup with a lid.

"What kind of medication are you on?" Katherine asked as she stirred the cocoa.

"Medication?"

"You know, little pills that come in all shapes, colors and sizes." She smiled teasingly. "From the pharmacy, also known as the *drug*store."

"Sure. Um, actually I'm not on any medication."

"Still, I'd better keep your cocoa unspirited," Katherine replied, recapping the bottle of amaretto she'd brought with the cocoa.

Paul sighed, knowing he couldn't put up a valid argument since he'd invented the concussion. Accepting the thick stoneware mug, his glance lingered longingly on the amaretto. But when he sipped the warm brew, he pulled back in surprise, expecting the usual insipid cocoa that came in packets, the kind he always avoided, preferring the bitter bite of black coffee. "This tastes great—not like the cocoa I'm used to."

Another look of puzzlement flickered over her face. "It's the way I always make it—" she gestured toward the firmly capped amaretto "—minus the added fuel." She tilted her head as she studied him. "You've always said you loved the way the European chocolate makes it taste like dessert."

He told himself to behave like Matthew. "Right. I guess I just forgot how good it was."

"No, that's not it."

His gaze flew to meet hers. Had she found him out?

"You're angling for the amaretto, but flattery won't get you anywhere, bud. I'm sure they told you concussions and alcohol don't mix. Talking up my cocoa won't help."

Paul barely managed to withhold a sigh of relief.

"Although reminding me about dessert is never a bad idea," she added, lifting her eyebrows suggestively.

Paul felt his stomach sink. Why couldn't she be a cold fish with a perpetual headache? But no, a smart mover wouldn't fail to kiss the breadwinner. He simply had to find a way to avoid her.

And that wasn't going to be easy since they were to share the same bed.

KATHERINE TRIED not to stare at Elliott as he moved awkwardly around the bedroom. He was behaving as if he'd never set foot in the place.

And it was more than just that. He acted like a stranger in his own skin, as though it no longer fit properly. His tall muscular build had always seemed so at ease. Yet he'd been skittish and jumpy ever since he'd come home, nothing like his normal self.

Katherine glanced at the dark hair with its unfamiliar cut, the bare upper lip. Even his blue eyes weren't quite the same. So much about him seemed different. But then, perhaps almost being killed did that to a person.

Suspecting Elliott had suffered more than he admitted, Katherine wondered if the trauma was as much emotional as physical. There was a haunted wary look in his eyes, one she'd never seen before.

Something primitive deep inside rang an answering need, but Katherine tamped it down. She didn't want him to change. She was more comfortable with the way he'd always been—fun, playful.

She wondered if he was viewing everything with fresh eyes, newly valuing what he'd previously taken for granted.

But surely the changes wouldn't last. No doubt he'd be back to normal by breakfast.

CHAPTER THREE

HURDLES. HIS PRODIGAL return, then meeting Dustin. They were a bitch, Paul decided, but he could handle them. Spending the night in his brother's bed with his brother's wife, however, was a hurdle of another nature.

He glanced toward the large breezy kitchen, making certain she was still cooking breakfast. He needed time alone, time to get a grip on how Matthew would behave.

And time to make a thorough search of the house.

The room he had glimpsed last night was indeed a study. He hoped it held the account books he wanted to examine. Having seen Katherine's puzzled looks, Paul wondered how long he could pull this off before she pitched him out on his identical face.

Katherine turned just then and, seeing him, waved. Halfheartedly he waved back. She gestured toward the dining room. So much for time alone.

Still, he needed to act the way Matthew would. Yawning, he stretched largely as he entered the dining room, spying a plate of steaming pancakes and an assortment of jellies and syrups. "Looks great. I'm starving."

"I was hoping you would be. That's why I made so much." She held up a skillet. "I also made your favorite."

"An omelette?" he asked with genuine pleasure.

Her smile faltered. "No. Eggs Benedict."

Paul wanted to kick himself. He should have realized Matthew's tastes might have changed. He reached toward his head, feigning sudden weakness. "Of course. Omelettes haven't been my favorite for quite a while."

She placed the pan on a trivet. "How do you feel this morning? You don't look too well."

"I guess I'm not back to my old self yet." That had been his explanation the previous night when he hadn't wanted to share anything more than a chaste kiss. If Matthew was alive, Paul certainly didn't want to find himself explaining why he'd slept with his wife.

And the sight of the eggs Benedict staring up at him like a pair of accusing eyes made his stomach feel as though he'd just eaten a load of lead. "You know, I'm really not as hungry as I thought."

Katherine stopped in the process of sliding fresh melon onto his plate. "Shouldn't you have a little something?"

"Just coffee for now. I can eat the eggs later if I get hungry—I'll pop them in the microwave."

"The microwave?" she uttered in a tone that indicated he'd suggested warming his breakfast in something unspeakably foul. "Later this will taste like warmed-over rubber."

"That's okay. I'm not picky."

Katherine's eyes widened. "Since when?"

Paul had the urge to thump himself on the side of his head. Of course, Matthew had always been a picky eater. Instead of the thump, Paul reached toward the "bump" on his head and drew his expression into a grimace.

Katherine dropped her questions, forgetting the line of conversation. "I shouldn't be making you talk. It probably makes your head hurt worse."

"Yes," he admitted, watching her through eyes scrunched up as though in pain. "The doctor said I'd have difficulty processing thoughts. Some things might seem unfamiliar."

"Like amnesia?" she asked in a horrified tone.

"Yes," he agreed, already having considered using amnesia as an excuse. "The doctor said I'd probably forget a lot of things—some minor, some possibly major."

One hand flew to her lips. "Oh!" Then Katherine's voice quieted, growing very small. "Do you remember me?"

In that instant Paul realized he was poised to set himself up well or break the act. "Somewhat."

"Somewhat?" she echoed in a disbelieving whisper.

"I know *who* you are," Paul improvised. "But there are big blocks I'm missing."

"Like...what we mean to each other?" she asked, her hands clutching the sides of the table until her knuckles whitened.

Again Paul wondered if this was an act. Had it occurred to Katherine that her husband might suspect she'd had some part in the accident?

Not certain he wanted her thinking in that direction, Paul decided to stall. He touched the top of his head a third time and grimaced.

She was all concern. "It's okay. Don't get stressed about anything else." She leaned forward, gently stroking his face. "I don't want you to worry. Everything will work out."

One way or another Paul was sure it would.

PAUL QUICKLY CHECKED OUT the interior of the small café, immediately spotting John Lewis, his contact. The natives were easily recognizable with their suntanned skin, casual clothing and easygoing manners. John, despite his efforts to blend in, still managed to stand out.

Sliding into the booth opposite his associate and longtime friend, Paul could see that the location for their meeting had been chosen wisely. The café was nearly deserted and the booth he'd selected was located at the far end of the room against the rear wall. John had already ordered coffee and pie for both of them.

"Elliott," John greeted him. "How's it going?"

Paul shrugged as he picked up his coffee. "I don't know much on this end." His fingers tightened on the thick ceramic mug, needing but dreading more news. "How about yours?"

"Not a lot." John's sympathetic gaze met his. "No more on Matthew, I'm sorry to report. We're still combing the coast, but nothing yet. Don't worry, the chief says we'll continue searching." John paused. "But we do have more information on the possible cause of the crash."

Paul cataloged the information about Matthew, steeling himself not to react. "And?"

"Looks like sabotage—just as you suspected. Wilkinson thought it could be engine failure, but now he's convinced it wasn't accidental."

Paul nodded, wondering if his mercurial brother could have possibly escaped a saboteur's bomb. "Wilkinson is the expert."

"Any new theories?" John asked him.

Paul shook his head, then dug his fork into the pie. "No one besides his wife had anything to gain from Matthew's death, as far as I can tell."

"Except you," John replied quietly.

Paul's head shot up and he had to refrain from letting his body follow. "What's that supposed to mean?"

"Cool down. I want you to consider the whole picture in case you're thinking of confronting the wife right away."

Since that was exactly what he'd been thinking of doing, Paul just said, "Such as?"

"Such as, who else would benefit? Didn't you and Matthew share the trust your parents left you?"

Paul nodded.

"Which positions you to inherit the entire thing."

Paul studied his associate. "The only way you would know that is if you'd seen a copy of the trust."

John lifted one shoulder in a shrug. "And you know how easily we obtained that."

"So I'm a suspect now?"

"No, we were just doing our homework. But if you throw this thing in the wife's face, she's liable to throw it right back."

Paul exhaled deeply. "Point taken."

"If you really think this woman is capable of cold-blooded first-degree murder, I'd say the element of surprise is crucial."

Paul pushed his dessert plate to the outer edge of the table and stood. "Agreed."

"In case you're right…" John's sober gaze didn't waver "…well, I'd watch my back if I were you."

CHAPTER FOUR

KATHERINE SMILED NERVOUSLY as Elliott entered the catering kitchens for the first time since his accident. As the chef of Combined Catering, Elliott was crucial to the operation. And this morning she'd told him just how crucial.

But once again he was acting strangely. He roamed the kitchen as though aboard a boat that listed. Worse, he looked as though he expected the galley to roll away at any moment. Instead of going straight to the menus as he always had, he watched the other employees: Carter, the sous-chef; cooks Alice, Ben and Frank; and the kitchen assistants.

Rather than watch her husband, Katherine tried to busy herself checking the day's orders. Yet her gaze continued straying toward him.

"Katherine?"

Taken off guard, she jumped before recovering. "I'm sorry, Ben. What is it?"

"What's up with Elliott?"

Katherine clutched her clipboard to her chest. "What do you mean?"

"He behaves as if he's never been in a kitchen before. You sure he's okay?"

Alice joined them. "He's acting really weird. I heard he took a pretty bad hit on the head."

Miserably Katherine agreed. "Yes, he did. To be honest, I'm not sure if he's completely well yet." She took a deep breath. "In fact, he has some amnesia."

"Some?" Ben questioned, sneaking a look at Elliott.

"Well, he remembers certain things, but he has big blocks that are missing," Katherine replied quietly, not wanting Elliott to notice they were talking about him.

"I thought amnesia victims forgot their names and people they know, not everyday stuff like reading or writing or cooking if you're a chef," Alice said.

Ben nodded. "That's what I thought, too."

Katherine frowned. "I don't really know. I guess it's different with every person. Besides, we don't know for sure that he's forgotten his skills in the kitchen."

Ben watched Elliott. "Sure looks like it."

Silently Katherine was forced to agree. At the moment Elliott was attacking some scallions as though he expected them to strike back. Just then he glanced up, catching her gaze on him. And he didn't look particularly pleased.

Were Ben and Alice right? Was it abnormal for Elliott to have forgotten the basic skills of his profession? Then she shook her head. She guessed Ben and Alice had gotten their information from television and movie mysteries—hardly reliable sources. Choosing to ignore what they'd said, Katherine walked over to Elliott.

She slipped a casual arm around his waist, trying not to be hurt when he stiffened. "Hey there. Want to go over some menus with me?"

He glanced down at the mangled vegetables, a whisper of relief coming over his face. "Sure." Wiping his hands on a nearby towel, he readily deserted the mess he'd made.

Katherine managed to smile as she met the questioning looks from the other employees as she and Elliott wound through the kitchen and entered the tiny space they'd carved out for an office. By mutual agreement most of the space in the building had been dedicated to the kitchen and prep areas.

She pulled out the folder with the week's orders, noticing that Elliott's eyes hadn't left her for a moment. "We have the Anderson and Fuller weddings, and the Montgomerys' twenty-fifth wedding anniversary." Katherine thumbed through the papers, then paused. "Here's a note about a funeral tomorrow—the call must have come in late yesterday after I left."

"We're catering a funeral?" Elliott asked skeptically.

"I know they're not your favorite, but it generates income and clientele as you always say."

"Hmm."

Katherine looked over the top of the folder at her husband. She wondered if he'd forgotten about that, too. She couldn't stave off the worry that he'd forgotten far more than he was letting on.

Then he grinned in typical Elliott fashion. "Funerals don't create *repeat* clientele," he quipped.

She couldn't resist smiling back, glad to see a flicker of his former self. "You're delightfully awful."

Alice stuck her head through the open doorway, interrupting the moment. "Katherine, the paper vendor is here—some mix-up about your order."

Regretfully she replaced the folder, wishing Alice hadn't chosen just then to intrude. "I'll go check on the order. Do you want to start on the menus, Elliott?"

With only the barest hesitation, he nodded, his smile still in place.

Katherine tried to conceal her anxiety as she escaped. She glanced back briefly, the unanswered question bombarding her: Would he ever be the same again?

PAUL'S GRIN FADED as he watched Katherine's retreat. Then he dropped his gaze to the orders. Menus? His idea of a meal was whatever he could microwave. So what did you serve at a wedding? Cake, he assumed. But that left a few holes in the menu, such as the main course. And for a funeral?

Nothing too perky, he guessed, pushing one hand through already disheveled hair.

Paul realized he was in way over his head. Once he and his twin had practically been inside each other's skins. It hadn't been a stretch to switch places when they were kids. Paul always believed he knew Matthew as well as he knew himself. It was unnerving to learn how much that had changed. It seemed their estrangement had severed part of their deep bond.

As he had since the plane had gone down, Paul thought again of why he and Matthew had become estranged—the woman who had come between them. Paul had loved Susan desperately. And he believed she'd loved him back, to the extent that she had agreed to marry him. Then she'd met his impulsive fun-loving twin. While Paul was on an extended assignment in South America, Matthew and Susan had begun dating.

Although Matthew later broke up with Susan and apologized to his twin, Paul never forgave him. He'd held him responsible for ruining his one true love. And despite Matthew's efforts to repair their relationship, Paul had stubbornly refused to bend. He had even accepted a transfer from Atlanta to Chicago to put more miles between them.

Only when Matthew called with the news of his marriage had Paul begun to yield. Still, he'd never said the words, never truly forgiven his brother. Paul's eyes flickered shut briefly. How much damage and time had he allowed to come between them? And why? Over a woman who had ultimately disappeared from both their lives. Paul didn't want Susan back—she had shown her true colors. However, despite the women Paul had dated since, he hadn't released the hurt, the feeling of betrayal. Instead, he had chosen to punish Matthew by staying aloof.

Now, amid Matthew's family and friends, Paul could see what he had lost, what he'd missed these past few years. Memories of their good times prior to the estrangement continued to assail him. Paul realized that he had no one to blame but himself. And as the days continued passing without word of Matthew, Paul was losing hope that there would be any new memories to create.

For the first time Paul was glad their parents had died when he and Matthew had been much younger. Parents shouldn't have to bury their child, and Paul was beginning to doubt there could be any other outcome.

Looking through the window, he could see that Katherine was still out of sight, so he decided to take a chance and search the desk. Pushing a pile of papers to the side, he spotted a small silver frame. The sight of his brother's grinning face unsettled him. With unsteady hands he reached out for the picture. Matthew's ready grin was something Paul needed to remember to do more often. No doubt everyone was wondering what had happened to it.

But it was agony to smile when he didn't know

Matthew's fate. And it was equal torture to impersonate his brother, especially for Katherine's benefit. Part of him wanted to shake the truth out of her. Another part of him hoped she had made his brother happy in what could have been his last months.

Absently Paul smoothed his fingers over the picture. All three faces in the picture were smiling: Matthew, Katherine and little Dustin. To the casual observer it was the portrait of a perfect family.

"Elliott?" Katherine's soft voice was questioning as she poked her head into the office.

Looking up, Paul could see that her gaze had landed on the picture he still held.

"Are you thinking back on happier times?" she asked quietly. Moving closer, she leaned across the desk to lay her hand atop his. "Don't worry. We'll get there again."

Paul felt a stab of mixed emotions. "I'm not sure about that." He put down the frame and picked up the order folder. "I seem to have lost my ability here, as well."

"Oh." Katherine's voice was small, then she cleared her throat. "That's all right. We can put Carter in charge of the kitchen until you're…until you're better. He's been champing at the bit to prepare his own menus and do his own take on the cuisine, anyway." She hesitated only slightly. "Of course we'll need to increase his salary. Carter's been insisting he needs a raise for some time—since he's always broke." Her eyes met Paul's, searching, then she added, "But of course, his promotion will only be temporary, until you're ready to take over the helm again."

"Why don't you take charge?" Paul asked, watching her. Did she have a distaste for an honest day's work?

Again Katherine's eyes clouded. "Because I'm a pastry chef, Elliott. As good as they are, I doubt if one of my tortes could pass for the main course."

"Of course," he replied, wishing he knew more, actually knew *anything* about the catering business. "I seem to have forgotten more than I realized."

"It's all right. We'll deal with it." Yet she looked tense, scattered. "I think for now I'd better talk with Carter, get these menus together. You could take a break and head over to the gym."

"A break? I just got here."

"Um, yes, well…"

"I'm not a two-year-old. I can entertain myself, even do some work. I can check the books, get the office in order." The lazy Carolina life-style mystified him. How did these people get anything done?

Katherine glanced around the crowded space as though seeing it for the first time. Then she shrugged. "If you want to clean up the office, that's fine. It's always seemed okay to me. It's not as though we spend much time in here."

"Maybe someone should," Paul suggested.

Her brows drew together. "Meaning?"

Paul remembered and then strove for a natural-looking grin. "Just that if I'm not much help in the kitchen right now, I can at least pull my weight by working to get the accounts straightened out."

The line between her eyes disappeared. "If you'd enjoy doing that…"

"I sure don't want to sit here and gather moss," he replied, looking again at the paper mountain around him. Then he caught her quizzical glance. Of course. Matthew would have been very content to blow off work. "The accident made me realize I'm not a kid anymore, Katherine. It's time I acted like it."

Her mouth formed a surprised "Oh." Recovering, she smiled. "If that's what you want." She gestured at the piles of paper on the desk. "There's certainly enough to keep you busy." She moved away, then turned back. "I know this is all very confusing. I can't even imagine how it must feel to have holes in your memory, but everyone wants to make this…transition as easy as possible for you. They love you. I love you."

Paul watched her through steady eyes. He couldn't form the words she waited to hear. He wanted to convincingly portray Matthew, but he couldn't tell this woman he loved her. Instead, he rose from behind the desk, put his hands on her upper arms and pulled her close for a moment. An enticing aroma of honey and flowers assailed him, along with her yielding softness. He attempted to ignore both. "Thanks, Katherine." Briefly he closed his eyes, shutting out the truth. "Soon everything should be back to normal. You'll see."

EVEN THOUGH A FEW DAYS had passed, Katherine still couldn't shake her concern. After checking the list of supplies, she shoved it aside. "I have to make sure this gets to the catering kitchens before morning."

"I can drop that off for you," Jessica offered. "I have an errand about a block away."

"No one's there. The place is locked."

"I can use the spare key you gave me," Jessica reminded her. "You don't need to be worrying about business right now."

"What should I worry about, instead? That I'm a stranger to my husband?"

"He didn't say that. He has some missing blocks and he's only been home a couple of days. Sounds to me like they could come back at any time."

Katherine smiled at her friend. "Is that your experience, Doctor?"

Jessica grinned. "Maybe I have seen too many episodes of 'Matlock' and 'Murder She Wrote.' But I still think you're making more of this than you should. I always heard that pressure to remember makes the amnesia even worse. What does the doctor say?"

Katherine frowned, remembering her conversation with Elliott. "I haven't actually talked to the doctor myself. Elliott doesn't seem to want me to."

Jessica tilted her head, studying her friend. "I know you want to make this all better, Katie, because that's who you are. You're a fixer. You want to fix your friends' problems and their friends' problems. Face it, you want to fix the world, but sometimes you have to let a man be a man."

"But he wasn't like this before!" Katherine blurted. "He liked it when I fixed things."

"Maybe almost dying made him want to take charge of his own life," Jessica replied sagely. "That's not a bad thing, you know."

"I know." Restless, Katherine stood up and began pacing the small office, pausing beside a window that boasted a glorious, if distant, view of the ocean. "He acts so differently, so grown up." She laughed at the ridiculousness of the words, then sobered. "Yes, I know how that sounds, but I don't care. I don't want to lose my carefree husband."

"Maybe you're not losing. Maybe you're gaining something better." Jessica hesitated. "A man who can be an equal partner, who can take an equal share of the load."

Katherine started to protest, then thought better of it. Jessica knew her well, knew that she'd had some concerns about Elliott's irresponsibility. He spent lavishly, then laughed off her worries.

Now Elliott had an uncharacteristic interest in the books—in fact, in everything that concerned the business. Long after she retired for the evening, he stayed in the study, immersed in the records and accounts. He would stay up so late that she would fall asleep before he came to bed. And often he slept in the study, explaining that he had fallen asleep while working. She remembered that before the accident he used to chase her up the stairs, eager to tumble into bed.

"Katie?"

Katherine pulled herself out of her reverie and grinned ruefully. "I sound as if I'm not grateful for Elliott's return, but I really am."

"Of course you are. I know how sick with worry you were when you thought Elliott wasn't coming home. But it's natural with his amnesia for him to act a bit differently."

"Do you see it, too?"

Jessica hesitated.

"I knew it!" Katherine pounced.

Jessica held up one hand. "Hold it! Yes, I see that he's not quite the same, but don't go ballistic on me. I had the feeling it was the amnesia thing. For a moment I felt as though he thought he had never seen me—like we were complete strangers. But then he seemed okay."

Katherine walked the length of the room, then stopped abruptly at the window. "Do you think amnesia can change a person's feelings?"

"How so?"

Katherine fiddled with the shutter. "Do you think it can make someone love less?"

Shocked, Jessica stared at her friend. "Did he say that?"

"Of course not. It's just…he doesn't seem as interested in me."

"Interested?" A light of understanding dawned in Jessica's eyes. "Romantically?"

Katherine nodded miserably.

"Is that what's worrying you?"

Katherine nodded again.

"Oh, Katie. The man almost died—that takes something out of a person. He probably spent a lot of time wondering what would happen to you and Dustin if he didn't make it. That's probably why he's so concerned about the business, about the responsibilities. And with the amnesia, maybe he's not as sure of himself in any arena, including the bedroom. Give him time, Katherine. Don't look for dents in his armor. Just be glad your white knight returned."

A remorseful Katherine took her friend's hand. "I can't believe how insensitive I've been. I know you would give anything to have Michael back, for him to have survived."

Jessica shook her head as though dispelling a torrent of painful memories, her voice shaky. "You're right. I'd take him back in a heartbeat, warts and all. But that's in the past and Michael won't ever be coming back. Those are the breaks." She squeezed Katherine's hand. "That's why I'm telling you not to bite Lady Luck on her elegant behind. You've done well by her."

"I know. And I am grateful, Jessica. I'll take Elliott however I can get him. Maybe you're right. Maybe I should be thinking of all the positives, instead of the negatives. I always did secretly wish he was a little more responsible."

"Then give him a chance to be," Jessica advised. "Don't insist on being the strong one. Lean for a change." She smiled wistfully. "When you can't anymore, you miss it."

Katherine fidgeted. "And you think the other... thing will come around?"

Jessica laughed. "I didn't realize you were such a sex maniac."

Flushing, Katherine concentrated on the toe of her sandal. "I'm not. It's just that Elliott always had an insatiable need. I can't help wondering what happened to it."

"It nearly got killed in an airplane crash. I think that deserves recovery time, just like his head."

Katherine considered this. "I hadn't thought about it that way."

Jessica smiled widely. "Besides, you can always dream up a romantic setting—it's practically what you do for a living. So what's to worry about?"

CHAPTER FIVE

THE TEDDY BEAR landed with a thump on Paul's lap. Dustin wasn't far behind. The child had just come home from Jessica's. As a commercial artist, Jessica worked out of her home, and she cared for Dustin, who was a playmate for her son, Brian.

Dustin's grin matched his enthusiasm. Paul was trying to hold the kid at a distance, but it was proving damn hard.

"Bobby Bear didn't mean to play rough," Dustin told him as he scrambled onto Paul's lap, staring at his head, clearly looking for the supposed wound.

"That's okay, tiger. I'm not so fragile." Even though he wanted to keep the child a stranger, Paul found himself securing Dustin on his lap. Didn't want the kid falling, he told himself. Still, he felt awkward with the toddler, unsure of what to say or do. "So, what did you do today?"

Dustin blinked, those huge eyes of his seeming to grow. "Me and Brian went to Zorak."

"Zorak?" Paul asked hesitantly. Was that an almost-four-year-old's pronunciation of something he should know?

"Sure. That's where the space monsters live."

"Oh." Paul considered this. "Do you know many space monsters?"

Dustin shook his head. "'Course not. They eat people—you musta knowed that."

"Can't say as I did," Paul admitted, intrigued by the little guy's tale in spite of himself. "Good thing you warned me. Why do you visit Zorak if the space monsters live there?"

Dustin looked at him in disbelief. "'Cause it's fun."

"Sure. Guess I forgot you have to do some stuff just for fun."

"You could go with us sometimes," Dustin offered. "But you'd hafta be a rider. Brian's always the pilot."

"Why's that?"

"'Cause he's older. He's five!" Dustin confided, clearly impressed.

"That old, huh? You sure he'd let a grown-up come along?"

Dustin scrunched his face in concentration. "I dunno. But Brian knows you got hurted and you act funny now."

Paul cleared his throat, suddenly alerted. "I act funny now?"

Dustin cocked his head. "Uh-huh. Not like before."

"Um…have you told anybody I act funny?"

"No. Mommy already knows."

Alarms started clanging at a ferocious rate. "She does?"

Dustin nodded his small head earnestly. "She says it's 'cause you got hurted and so we have to play careful with you."

"Oh. Anything else?"

Dustin pulled his brows together. "Like what?"

Paul shrugged, striving for a casual tone. "Nothing special. Just anything else Mommy might have said."

Suddenly Paul was appalled at himself. He was asking the child to rat on his mother, and with the information Paul could completely change Dustin's life. "Never mind, Dustin, it doesn't matter. Tell you what—when I was a little boy, we didn't know how to get to Zorak, but I knew how to play soldiers or cowboys."

"Cowboys!" Dustin decided in an instant, grinning as he struggled to get down.

Paul helped him, sharing the child's smile as he scampered toward his room to get some toys.

Within a few minutes Dustin was back, his arms so full of toys he could barely see around them.

Laughing, Paul reached over to unload him. "Hey, tiger, are you under there somewhere?"

Dustin's head bobbed in assent, as he chewed on his lip in concentration. "Uh-huh. You wanna be the cowboy or the Indian?"

"Which one do you want to be?"

"Indian," Dustin answered promptly. "He gets to wear the feathers."

"Sounds fair to me. When we were kids, my brother and I used to take turns. That way we got to play everything from cowboys to Martians."

Dustin frowned. "What's Martians?"

Paul laughed. "Sort of like the space monsters on Zorak, but they don't eat people."

"You don't talk about your brother much." Katherine surprised him, her voice coming from the doorway of the living room.

Paul glanced over at her, noticing her bare feet. That was why he hadn't heard her come into the room. He wondered if she'd done that on purpose, so she could eavesdrop. He also wondered how long she'd been standing there. "Well, we…" What in the hell had Matthew told her? Estranged, he thought.

"I know. You said you'd been on the outs for a while, with only a vague hope for reconciliation." She crossed to him and rested a hand on his shoulder, her eyes thoughtful. "I'm just glad you remember you have a brother."

Thrown off guard, Paul felt as though he'd just piloted himself into the fantasy world of Zorak. "Well…"

She smiled again, that rainbow burst of light. "Maybe everything else is close behind." Her fingers ruffled his hair, which was growing to an unaccustomed length. Since his return, it was only one of many subtle changes. "You know what? We haven't had a picnic for dinner in ages. What do you say, guys? The great outdoors?"

Dustin was already jumping up and down, so Paul nodded.

"Super." Katherine headed out of the room, then paused, meeting Paul's eyes. "In case I haven't told you today, I'm awfully glad you're home." Without waiting for his reply, she disappeared into the kitchen.

Paul heard her humming in the next room as she opened cabinets, then rummaged through the pantry. At the same time he felt something pressing at his knees and glanced down. Dustin was pushing a toy rifle at him.

"Cowboys!" Dustin insisted.

"Right, tiger. I think we'd better go outside, though. Your mom probably doesn't let you have horses in the house."

Dustin giggled in reply and Paul found himself warming again. He told himself it was because he liked having a receptive audience to his dubious humor, not because of the small hand curled so trustingly in his. As they headed outside, it occurred to him that a man never felt taller than when walking hand in hand with a child.

"CURRY?" PAUL ASKED. "I don't think I ever had curry on a picnic before."

"I was going for a theme—you know, to fit with cowboys and Indians."

"Isn't curry from India, a place decidedly lacking in cowboys?"

She threw a linen napkin at him. "Okay, okay. You can see now why I couldn't be the chef. I don't think the guests would understand my themes, either."

"Is Dustin going to eat curry?" Paul asked. It didn't seem like something a little kid would like.

Katherine produced some sandwiches. "Peanut butter and jelly. I think that'll keep him happy. Unless you were thinking maybe beef jerky for trail grub in keeping with the *theme*." She held up some other bags. "Chips, granola and, of course, his favorite—brownies, since he's not a fan of my éclairs or napoleons."

Paul decided to take advantage of her relaxed guard. "Help fill in the gaps—why did you decide to be a pastry chef?"

"You mean, instead of a *real* chef?" Katherine retorted, her smile and raised brows taking the sting out of her words. Before he could reply, she waved her hands in dismissal. "It's okay. I'm used to the kitchen class system. As you well know, many pastry chefs look down their noses at you guys, too!"

At the moment Paul was feeling the inexplicable desire to tap her petite and very appealing nose. Perhaps it was because she kept twisting her face in a flirty teasing fashion. Distracted, he grunted a reply.

"Somehow I don't see you as being easily intimidated."

"Exactly," she replied, surprising him. "So why should I pretend to like something I don't? My passion has always been pastries. Give me a torte, tiramisu, or cheesecake any day. Who wants to concoct vegetable or meat dishes when you can create a fabulous dessert?" Katherine's eyes grew dreamy. "How often has someone raved over the carrots? But the dessert, that's another matter. That's what everyone remembers!"

Her enthusiasm was infectious and Paul didn't have to manufacture an answering smile. His cell phone rang suddenly and he suppressed a flinch. He'd forgotten to turn it to vibrate only.

Katherine turned a startled face in his direction. "What was that?"

"Just the cell phone," Paul said dismissively, knowing he would let it ring rather than answer it. No doubt it was one of the operatives trying to make contact.

"When did you get a cell phone?" she asked incredulously. "And why? You said you'd never own an electronic tether!"

Was there no end to the differences between him and his brother?

Paul sighed. "I know. But if I'm going to work on the business end of things, I need to be accessible. And smoke signals won't cut it."

Katherine reached to caress the line of his jaw.

"You don't have to take on the whole world for us, you know. It's enough that you're here for Dustin and me." She blinked away the tears that filled her eyes and began spilling down her cheeks. "I never knew before how very important that is."

Without volition he wiped the tears away, smoothing them over velvet skin, his fingers lingering near the line of her lips. In that instant she seemed so very believable. With a start he pulled back. Was this how Matthew had been sucked in? Had he been taken in by her huge violet eyes and quivering lips?

Dustin came running back from the slide, where he'd been playing, and moments later Katherine tilted her face heavenward, pointing out the shapes in the clouds to him.

Ignoring the endless sweep of sky, the evocative call of the gulls, Paul watched her, determined she wouldn't beguile him, as well.

THE DAYS CONTINUED to pass, but the nights seemed to drag.

Tonight the moon was full to bursting, sending lush tendrils of light into the darkness. Katherine watched the shadows creep down the flowered wallpaper, animating the cabbage roses. The room was the first she had redecorated since she and Elliott had married.

She had always dreamed of an English country cottage, and Elliott hadn't minded the flowers, the lace, the antiques or the sea-washed pastels she had chosen. He had told her, with that endless grin of his, that his mind was on other things besides curtains and lace when he entered that particular room. As long as she was in the bedroom, he'd said, she could add anything else she wanted.

Katherine longed to see that grin again, the grin that seemed to have disappeared with his plane crash. She should have been asleep hours earlier, but her mind refused to take that escape. She reached out across the expanse of empty mattress, her hand closing convulsively around the soft cotton coverlet. Once again Elliott had chosen to stay up late in the study. Why did he prefer the company of dry accounts to...to her? she wondered, a hot tear slipping beneath nearly closed lids.

Now he seemed to avoid her touch nearly as much as he avoided her. Restlessly Katherine tossed back the covers. The room seemed to be closing in on her; it felt too warm, despite the cooling breezes dancing in from the ocean.

She swallowed a sob, turning to bury her face in a pillow. Had he realized that a single mother and a small child were a huge burden? One he needn't have assumed, one that was now choking him? The tears that had threatened now escaped, along with the sobs she could no longer contain.

Vaguely she heard the careful creak of the door as it opened, the hesitant footsteps approaching the bed. But, unable to stop the emotions racking her,

Katherine buried herself more deeply in the pillow, trying to muffle the sounds of her distress.

"Katherine?" Elliott's voice was hesitant, uncertain. "What's wrong?"

She could only shake her head. What if this was the beginning of the end? She had faced too many endings already. She was uncertain she could face another.

"What is it?" Elliott sat on the bed and leaned over her, his arms flanking her, trapping her.

Katherine didn't want to look at him, but he was gently turning her to face him. "I can't…" She tried. "I can't…"

"You can tell me," he prompted, his voice mild, uncensoring. "Did you have a bad dream?"

She shook her head, tasting the salty wash of hot tears as they slid over her lips. "No, I wasn't asleep."

"Then what?" he asked, his hand awkwardly smoothing the tangle of her hair.

"I want us back," she finally blurted, the tears nearly choking the words.

"*I'm* back," he replied cautiously.

"But not all the way back," Katherine said, her voice raw with emotion.

"I don't know what you mean."

"You never used to stay up in the study all night!" she cried.

"I'm going over the books, I told you—"

"I know what you said." She broke in. "But I

can't believe that's all. You…you stay away from me.''

He drew back slightly. ''It's been hard for me since the accident.''

Katherine hesitated, her heart wrenching painfully. She was afraid to ask, but had to know. ''Is it me?''

Once again he sounded cautious. ''What do you mean?''

She agonized over revealing what was left of her shattered emotions, to lay bare the secrets of her soul, yet she had to know. ''Am I ugly to you now? Are you wishing you hadn't taken us on—Dustin and me?''

She heard the muffled curse, then felt Elliott's hand as he took hers.

''Of course not.'' Again he smoothed her hair. ''Have you looked in the mirror lately? I don't think you'll see anyone ugly there.''

Her eyelids fell briefly, then opened so she could study his face. He looked so serious! No grin to shrug away the problems, no teasing to dismiss unwanted thoughts. ''I'm not sure what I should be seeing. What *you're* seeing.''

His eyes met hers and in the low light Katherine wondered if she imagined their darkening. His voice was husky. ''That hasn't changed.''

''I need you,'' she admitted, scared to voice the thought, afraid not to. ''Don't you want me anymore?''

She saw the flash of uncertainty that even the dim light couldn't hide.

"It's not a matter of want..." he replied finally.

Their faces were close, his merely a handbreadth away. Desperately needing that connection, Katherine reached out to caress his jaw, then she twined her fingers in the hair that curled around his collar. With practiced ease, she found his lips. But there the familiarity ceased.

Silken heat infused her as their mouths met. Instead of easing into the slowly awakening path of desire that she was accustomed to, a whipcord of intensity shook her, the reverberation as unsettling and electric as it was unfamiliar.

His hands moved slowly over her arms, traveling to her waist, resting on the curve of her hip, each move creating stunning awareness. It was as though this was the first time he'd touched her, but even more. She didn't remember the electricity, the shocking heat that was consuming her. It had been some time, true, but where had this come from?

If she didn't know it was impossible, she would have sworn this was the touch of a stranger, an incredibly exciting stranger. Shaken, she drew back slightly, hearing the fevered rush of her own breathing—and his.

Her mouth was dry, her chest heaving in anticipation, the pulse at her throat leaping out of control. She extended an eager, yet shaky hand, expecting to feel the crush of his chest against hers, the length of his body pressed to hers.

The sudden springing of the mattress as Elliott rose was an equal shock. Which made his words that much more difficult to interpret.

"You're truly beautiful, Katherine, and that's something that will never change."

Her eyes widened as she watched him leave the room, then heard the tread of his footsteps as he retreated down the stairs. Alone in the dark with her own thoughts, she wondered if either of them would sleep that night—or together again. And why her husband had chosen to walk away.

CHAPTER SIX

THE NIGHTS FOLLOWING Katherine's outburst were now fraught with tension. Unable to cross that line, yet unwilling to hurt her further, Paul continued to use work as an excuse to avoid sharing her bed. But sleep was becoming more difficult for him, as well. He took advantage of the post-midnight hours to search the study thoroughly.

One night, when he tried to open the bottom drawer of the desk, Paul felt it stick. Stubbornly he pulled harder and it released with a thump. Puzzled, he glanced down. What had caused the thumping sound? It was as if something had dropped to the floor.

Pulling the drawer free from its track, he reached inside the desk frame, patting the floor, searching. He was ready to withdraw his hand when his fingertips grazed the edges of a thick wad of papers. His arm was already fully extended, so he couldn't quite get a grasp. He rose, then searched for and found a letter opener. Using it like a dragline, he scooted the papers close enough so he could get his hand around them.

Realizing he might well be reeling in Matthew's

old black book or something equally useless, Paul braced himself to be disappointed. He brought the papers up to the desk surface, beneath the light of a vintage art deco lamp.

Disappointment wasn't what he felt. As he skimmed the small type, he recognized that the documents were insurance papers. Life insurance. In Matthew's name.

His eyes widened as he read the amount. Matthew had been insured for a substantial amount. With grim purpose he flipped through the papers looking for the beneficiary.

Katherine Crowden Elliott.

With Matthew dead she stood to gain nearly half a million dollars, in addition to the entire business. More than enough motive for murder.

Regardless of tears—or beauty—Paul knew he was on track. And from what he could see, that track led to only one person. Involuntarily his eyes lifted toward the ceiling. And it wouldn't do to ever forget that.

KATHERINE STUDIED the man on Jessica's arm. Clearly her friend was taken with him, but Katherine wasn't sure what she thought of Rod Dennison. Tall and blond, he was handsome enough, in a slick sort of way.

Katherine widened her smile to include him as he emptied his drink. She tried to ignore his enthusiasm for the free drinks and, instead, thought about the evening's focus. "The benefit seems to be going well. The children's hospital should meet their goal if the momentum continues."

"Great gig," Rod answered, plucking another glass of wine from a passing waiter. "Jessica told me you're the caterer."

Katherine kept her smile in place. "Yes, it's a working party."

"Nothing wrong with that," Rod answered, tipping his glass to her. "Why not get paid to party?"

Why not indeed?

Jessica smiled at him fondly. "You always see the positive side of things."

"I've worked my share of parties," Rod told them. "Bartending."

"Oh, I didn't realize that," Katherine replied.

"Katherine's always looking for an extra bartender," Jessica said, obviously enchanted with him.

Katherine wasn't sure she was glad Jessica had shared that bit of information. "Crab puff?"

"My favorite," Jessica responded with a smile. "And yours are the best."

"Surprised you don't have something more original for appetizers," Rod commented after swallowing one. "Crab puffs are kinda 'been there, done that,' you know?"

Yet he seemed to be knocking them back fast enough, Katherine noted as he reached for a few more. She gritted her teeth against the slight. "Perhaps you'll find the main course more inventive."

"No offense," Rod told her. "Just that Jessica's been bragging about you and Elliott. Says you're the best. I thought your stuff would be on the cutting edge."

The man had a way of making even an apology sound like an insult, Katherine thought. Glancing at Jessica, she spotted her anxiety, recognized her desire to please. Katherine tactfully let the comment pass.

"As Katherine said, the main course is the place for creativity," Jessica inserted hastily. Rod took her hand and pulled her toward the dance floor. Jessica sent Katherine an apologetic look as they walked away.

Knowing how lonely Jessica had been since her husband's premature death, Katherine tried not to judge. Rod was probably a perfectly acceptable man who occasionally put his foot in his mouth at parties. It happened.

"Why the scowl?" Elliott asked from her side, surprising her. Completely focused on Jessica and Rod, she hadn't heard him approach.

"Oh, was I scowling?" Katherine forced her features into neutral.

"Yep. Looks as if you want to skewer someone out there."

"Maybe I do," she replied.

He lifted his brows. "That was candid."

"Oh, I suppose I don't mean it. It's that guy Jessica's with."

"Rod?" he asked, his gaze following hers and singling them out of the crowd.

"Yes. I'm not sure what to think of him."

"Why?"

Katherine paused. "He just seems too polished—like he's not real. And Jessica needs someone who's real, someone who can appreciate how wonderful she is."

Paul reached for a stack of linen napkins. "Isn't that up to Jessica?"

"Of course. But I've seen what she's gone through the past few years. Losing her husband so young in that accident…"

"Her husband died?" Elliott asked, sounding shocked.

Another piece of Elliott's history apparently lost, Katherine realized.

"Yes. It was tragic and his death nearly killed her. It's taken forever for her to date again. I hope Rod doesn't hurt her."

"And you think he will?" Elliott asked, a strange shadow in his eyes.

"I don't know. He just seems too…well oiled." She sneaked another look at the couple.

"Well oiled?" Paul repeated, amusement coloring his voice. "Is that a female term for something we men don't want to know?"

"Ha! As if you don't know what I mean. I'm afraid he's a mover, a smooth operator, a…a…"

"Snake-oil salesman?" Paul provided.

"You're just being a man!" she accused.

"Guilty. But I have a hard time outrunning that label."

Katherine smiled finally, realizing he was teasing her. "It's been a long time since you've done that."

His smile remained easy. "What?"

"Teased me," she replied, grinning. "I was beginning to think it was lost to the past."

His smile wavered briefly, then slipped back into place. "You don't want me to take myself so seriously?"

She studied him. "That's hard to answer. I've missed your lighter side, but I am impressed with the changes you've made in the business."

"Impressed?" he echoed.

Katherine nodded. "I hated being in debt, always worrying about the finances. But it doesn't look like I'll have to worry anymore, so yes, I guess I'm impressed."

"But I'm no snake-oil salesman?"

Katherine laughed in spite of her concern for Jessica. "I guess I am getting kind of carried away. Rod's probably okay, just a little on the superficial side. But Jessica's so…special. She deserves the best."

"And you don't think Rod's part of that elite group—the oh, two or three percent of the male population who aren't movers or smooth operators?"

Without blinking, she elbowed him smartly.

"Very funny, chum. I wasn't planning to turn this into a male-female battle."

"Didn't sound like that from my side of the battlefield."

She winced slightly. "Am I that obvious?"

His smile was smooth, rather than teasing. "Only to someone who knows you well."

Katherine's eyes softened, and a warm glow suffused her face. "And that would be you."

The laughter in his eyes faded, replaced by something she couldn't quite fathom. Something uncharacteristically grim. What had befallen her Peter Pan in that crash?

"Elliott," she said gently, taking his arm, "it doesn't matter, you know, how bad the accident makes you feel, I mean. We can talk about it. I know things are different. *You're* different."

His head jerked up. "What do you mean?"

"It's not easy to explain," she murmured, caught by the intensity in his eyes. Where had this come from? This scintillating edge that made her pulse quicken. A sigh that originated somewhere way down deep emerged.

"You sound tired," he said, backing away.

"No, I—" she began to protest.

"I'll check on the line, see how the carving station's holding up...oh, and the dessert table." The odd look on his face twisted into a grin. "There probably aren't any of your crepes left. They're going like hotcakes," he quipped.

His attempt at humor couldn't dampen her heightened awareness. Although it was crazy, Katherine felt as though she was caught in that first flush of passion, as though anticipating their first touch. How could that be? His was a touch she knew well.

Why then, did her skin tingle when he was near? As Elliott walked away, she stared at the familiar lines of his body, wondering why nothing about him seemed familiar any longer.

PAUL SLID ONTO the booth's vinyl-covered bench. The café's discreet neon sign lit up the corner of the window while a chalkboard advertised the daily specials. But Paul wasn't looking for something to eat. He was here to meet John Lewis.

Paul tried to prepare himself for the worst. Matthew may have been found. Although hope was all but extinct, he wanted to believe his mercurial twin could beat the worst odds. Paul rested his forehead on one upraised hand. What if this was the one time Matthew had failed?

"Elliott?" John Lewis said quietly, one solid hand resting briefly on Paul's shoulder. Then he sat down opposite him. "You okay?"

"Yep. So, you have some news?"

John wore a noncommittal expression. "I'm afraid it's not about what you want to hear."

"Then nothing about Matthew?"

John shook his head.

Paul didn't know whether to be relieved or disappointed.

"Sorry," John said sympathetically, allowing the rare emotion to infuse his voice for a moment before assuming its usual blandness. "We don't know any more about Matthew."

It may have been foolish, but Paul allowed himself to feel a rush of relief at the temporary reprieve. "Then what?"

John paused. "We have some more information on Katherine."

Paul swallowed, bracing himself, wondering how bad it would be. "And?"

"It's not good. She and a partner owned a restaurant in Charlotte. It was on the verge of bankruptcy when a fire leveled the place."

Paul met his friend's eyes. "Let me guess. The insurance paid off."

John nodded. "Big time. Enough to clear their debts and provide some handsome seed money."

"Do you have a line on the partner?"

"Not yet." John hesitated. "But the restaurant was Katherine's inspiration."

As the catering business had been. Paul remembered the pride in Matthew's voice when, during their brief phone conversation, he'd described Katherine's expertise. He'd been convinced she had the business savvy to take them both far.

Well, Matthew had been half-right. At this point it looked as though she'd engineered him far, far out of the picture. Paul cleared his throat. "Was there an investigation?"

"Not then, but one's been instigated. Of course, the trail is pretty cold. But we should know in a few weeks if there was anything suspicious about the fire."

Paul bent his head for a moment, needing to know, yet dreading to ask. "Is the partner alive?"

"As far as we know." John hesitated again. "But he's dropped out of sight. Way out of sight."

"So he could be dead," Paul surmised, hating to take the leap, but knowing he had to be realistic.

"Hey, hold on there, buddy. That's a hell of an assumption. I said he's out of sight. We don't know he's dead."

Paul's voice was grim. "And we don't know he isn't. People have a funny way of disappearing around Katherine."

"She breaking her facade?" John asked, after accepting the coffee the waitress brought, then making sure she was out of earshot.

"Not exactly. She's still portraying the perfect wife, mother, concerned friend and likable employer."

"Doesn't exactly sound like Lizzie Borden," John observed.

"No. But all of Lizzie's neighbors thought she was a sweet young thing. Goes to show that appearances aren't everything."

"How about from your end?" John asked. "You uncover anything?"

Paul hesitated. "Can you do me a favor, John?"

His friend nodded. "Sure. What is it?"

Again Paul hesitated, this time visibly. "Can you find out who the father of Katherine's child is and where he is? Oh, and if there are any court orders regarding support, custody, that sort of thing?"

"You think she nabbed him illegally?" John asked.

"Not exactly. Could you just go along with me on this one? I don't have anything really solid. I just need some background info."

"You got it." John paused. "I'm guessing this has to do with the kid's future if you take his mother out of the picture."

"Yeah, pretty much. Oh, and can you see if her parents are still alive, any siblings? Goes to the first issue, but it would also help my cover. I'm running blind here. I used to think Matthew and I could trade places in the blink of an eye and not miss anything. Not so."

"Don't sound so down about it. That's part of aging, especially in our line of work. None of us are as close to family as we'd like to be. Nothing to beat yourself up about."

"Matthew and I are twins. That's not the average sibling bond. It's a deeper bond than most married couples share."

"Then it will help you solve this, Elliott. It'll

come back to you—how Matthew thinks, acts. That's something no background check can do for you. And it's what's going to help your brother.''

Paul smiled wearily. ''I know you're right. But as time passes, I can't believe we're going to have good news about Matthew.''

''Not unless he really does have amnesia,'' John suggested. ''It's possible.''

''And it's possible to win the Irish Sweepstakes,'' Paul responded evenly. ''I'm not counting on that, either.''

''That's just being smart.'' John met his gaze. ''The other is a matter of hope and faith, my friend. And both are pretty valuable right now.''

Paul picked up his own coffee mug, ignoring the breakfast he'd ordered. ''I suppose you're right.''

''Not going to eat?'' John asked, gesturing toward Paul's untouched plate. ''Looks like you've dropped some weight.''

Paul glanced down at his torso, drawing his brows together. ''Maybe. Haven't thought about it.''

''Since you're living with a chef, she's liable to notice it,'' John said. ''You might want to start eating again.''

Paul gazed in distaste at the food. ''I can't seem to stomach much these days.''

''This something to do with your brother being a chef?''

Paul smiled wryly. ''Is this what you learned in psych 101?'' Then he waved one hand in easy dismissal. "I know I'm depressed. I also know I'm focused. And I know that's a lethal combination, but I don't intend to starve myself in grief. I have to eat to keep up appearances when I'm with Katherine. That's more than enough."

John shrugged, meeting his friend's eyes. "Okay, no feeding tube for now."

Paul nodded, wondering what John was leaving unsaid. "And?"

"I'll repeat my earlier advice. Until we learn what happened to Katherine's partner, don't let your guard down." John met Paul's eyes with grim purpose. "Not for a second."

CHAPTER SEVEN

KATHERINE SLOWLY REPLACED the telephone receiver. Another hang-up call. She could never remember a time when there had been so many. And they seemed to happen only when *she* answered the phone. She'd asked Elliott, and although a shadow had passed over his face, he said he hadn't gotten any odd calls or hang ups. She hadn't felt comfortable pushing any further.

A peculiar itch was working its way through her system. An itch born of suspicion.

"Katherine?" Jessica asked from across the room. "Everything okay?"

She hesitated. "I'm not sure."

Jessica rose from the wicker chair. "What is it?"

"This is going to sound stupid…"

"So?" Jessica smiled encouragingly. "Haven't I confided a lot of stupid-sounding things to you?"

Katherine laughed weakly. "I guess so." She pushed back a wayward lock of hair. "It's just that as I think about saying this out loud…well, I sound like the wife from a drippy movie-of-the-week. The wife who mistrusts her husband's every move."

Jessica's expression turned to one of concern. "You want to be a little clearer?"

Katherine fiddled with the tapestry runner on the sofa table. "Well, since Elliott's accident, he has all sorts of meetings. You know how he's always been—just mention the word meeting and he'd disappear. And I'm not sure exactly what the meetings are about." She frowned, her hands falling still momentarily. "And these phone calls…" She met Jessica's eyes. "Hang ups. And the caller waits to hear who answers before they disconnect. I know this sounds ridiculous, but I can't help wondering if it's a woman."

Jessica picked up a mug of tea and brought it to Katherine. "You don't sound ridiculous. You sound like a normal woman with a normal amount of jealousy. But I really believe that the meetings are just business meetings and that the phone calls are a coincidence." She smiled. "And let's be sensible. Elliott works long hours. The rest of the time he's here with you and Dustin. When would he have found time to meet someone else?"

Katherine took a sip of tea, then glanced out the window toward the gently cresting ocean waves. "Good point. But I still don't understand the calls." She glanced back at the telephone. "Why did they suddenly start now?"

"Maybe someone's gotten hold of a wrong number and they're too stubborn to give up." Jessica hesitated. "Or, I hate to even mention this, but the accident received a lot of press. And that sometimes makes weirdos come out of the woodwork.''

Katherine paused, studying her friend's face. ''Did that happen when Michael died?''

Jessica nodded. ''It was something I never figured out. There were all kinds of crank calls. And salesmen—like I was in the mood to do a lot of buying, but I guess they were under the misconception I had insurance money to burn.'' She took a deep breath. ''I even had people calling to report they'd seen Michael after I'd buried him. What I'm saying, Katie, is it takes all kinds.''

''Did you have hang ups, too?'' Katherine asked softly, hating to probe that pain-filled time in her friend's life, yet needing to know.

Jessica shrugged. ''Probably. I remember thinking several times that I should change the phone number. But in the end it didn't matter all that much.'' She left the rest unsaid. It hadn't mattered because her husband had died, and without him nothing really mattered.

Katherine felt a wash of emotions. ''I'm sorry, Jessica. You're right. I should focus on being glad Elliott's alive, not worrying about this other silly stuff.''

''I didn't say that.''

''You didn't have to. The truth has a way of making itself heard.'' Katherine took another sip of the calming tea. ''Besides, I didn't mean to pick at your scabs. I guess I've had this brewing in my mind and it just sort of erupted.''

"You know better, Katie," Jessica chided. "You don't have to edit what you tell me. If this has been bothering you, you should have said something."

"I feel pretty stupid about the whole thing. I hate it when I hear about other women acting like this. I always wonder why they don't trust their husbands—or if they don't, why they don't confront them, get things out in the open."

Jessica's brow quirked. "You tried that?"

Katherine smiled sheepishly. "I've stuck to the complacent-wife mold so far."

"You'll know if there's a right time to say something, or if this is one you just keep under your hat."

Katherine's expression was rueful. "At this rate I'm going to need a six-foot-tall top hat."

"That bad?"

"I loved Elliott just the way he was, but now he's forceful, confident…"

"More attractive?" Jessica suggested.

Katherine felt warmth seep into her cheeks. "I guess it sounds silly, but this new edge he has…actually it's more exciting."

"That doesn't sound like such a bad thing."

"No. But I wonder what happened to everything that used to matter to him. It's almost as though he's avoiding anything at all to do with food preparation."

"Maybe, in some weird way, it's tied to his fear of what happened."

"I don't get it." Katherine shook her head. "He was flying, not cooking, when he had the accident."

"Not that exactly," Jessica protested. "But maybe his fear is connected to the set of memories that are close to what happened that day, something he's not comfortable with yet."

Katherine's eyes widened. "Do you think he feels that way about me, too? After all, I'm a big part of that time, the one he seems to want to forget."

"Jeez, Katie, I didn't mean for you to make a leap like that!"

"But it makes sense, doesn't it, Jessica?" Katherine set her mug down. "If he wants to forget the pain of that day, I'm a walking reminder. One he can't get away from day or night—unless he goes to meetings, ones that don't have anything to do with business."

"Oh, Katie, that was the worst leap yet!"

But Katherine wasn't seeing her friend. Instead, staring out the window, she could see the plane crash, Elliott's uncertainty when he returned. Soberly she turned toward her friend. "No, I'm afraid I'm finally facing the truth."

THE STAR-STREWN NIGHT SKY outdazzled the lights strung around the elaborate reception area. Waves from the bay lapped against the pilings that supported the building's impressive proportions. A Victorian delight, the house for the reception had clapboard siding, cupolas and a widow's walk. It was a setting designed to enchant, a romantic fantasy that promised to add luster to weddings and anniversaries.

And as the caterers, Paul and Katherine's contribution to this fantasy was to make sure the food and libation flowed smoothly, that the gourmet treats appeared effortlessly, that the glasses of champagne never emptied. It was illusion and packaging. It was stuff and nonsense. But their clients ate it up—figuratively and literally.

Paul had been watching Katherine for the better part of the evening. Dressed in some sort of lace-and-silk confection, she looked as though she could be the bride, her face aglow, eyes sparkling, a ready smile leaping to her lips time and again.

Now she approached, her hands filled with a heavy tray of soiled dishes.

Automatically he took it from her. "There's no need for you to haul around the heaviest stuff here," he admonished.

She shrugged. "I'm strong. It doesn't hurt me."

"You're not one of the guys," he continued, surprising both of them.

For a moment she froze, her wide-eyed gaze catching his. Then her hands ran nervously down the sides of her dress. "I guess I'm not." She pushed self-consciously at the long curly hair that spilled over her shoulders. In that instant she looked like some fey creature—all lace and silk, ivory skin and a cloud of hair.

"Try to remember that," he added lamely, his own concentration shot to hell as he shoved the dishes onto a waiting cart.

Again her hands fluttered before falling uselessly to her sides. "I will."

Unable to halt the motion, he gently tucked a lock of hair behind her ear. A small diamond earring winked at him, reflecting the moonlight as aptly as an ocean wave.

"Oh." Katherine sighed the word, a breathy exclamation that captured so much more than the mere utterance.

"Elliott! Katherine!" Ben called as he approached.

Frozen in their own tableau, it took them several moments to break apart. But even as the cook approached, Paul couldn't completely sever his concentration. He realized that given a few more minutes, he might have been unable to resist the urge to pull her close, to see if she felt as good as she looked.

Katherine, seeming ruffled for the first time that evening, turned to Ben. "What is it?"

"Carter's all bent out of shape. Says we don't have enough oysters and the mangoes aren't ripe."

Shaking her head as though to clear it, Katherine glanced at Ben. "Can't he improvise? Like Elliott always did?"

At her words Ben turned to look at Paul.

Paul concealed a flinch. Naturally they expected him to jump in and whip up something wonderful. But, of course, that wasn't going to happen. "I'll drive back to the kitchens," he said, "grab some oysters, see if we have some other mangoes. Ben, check with Carter and see what other fruit will work if the mangoes are all too hard. I'll call you on my cell while I'm driving so we won't lose too much time." Striding away, he didn't catch the matching looks of amazement.

"He's going to call en route?" Ben asked, his voice conveying incredulousness. "I didn't think Elliott even knew how to work a cell phone."

"Well, he's undergone some changes since the accident," Katherine murmured.

"Changes, hell. It's like the body snatchers captured him. It's downright spooky."

"Do me a favor, Ben. Don't tell Elliott you feel that way."

"Any reason why?"

Katherine glanced after Elliott. "I'm afraid a lot more has changed than he wants to let on." She sighed, stifling her own frustration. "And I don't think he wants us to know just how much."

PAUL SIFTED THROUGH the remnants of the wreckage. It was a pitifully small collection. Their plane hadn't been huge, but certainly far more should have been recovered. How could he summon even a shred of hope for his brother when so little had remained of their plane?

He bent his head, hiding his reaction from his fellow agents. *Oh, Matthew, this can't be all there is. It can't be over like this. Not even one more grin to share.*

John Lewis cleared his throat. "Elliott, I know it doesn't look good..."

Paul waved the words away. "I see how it looks."

"The chief isn't prepared to drop the investigation yet."

Paul released a breath he hadn't realized he was holding. *If there was even the smallest hope that Matthew was alive...* His voice was husky as he replied. "I may be chasing ghosts here, but I'm damned glad the chief sees fit to continue the investigation."

John clapped a sturdy hand on Paul's shoulder. "We're all in on this one until we find out some answers. If Matthew's wife wasn't behind the sabotage, that leaves a wide-open field of suspects."

Paul shook his head, remembering his brother's charisma, his talent for creating friends, not enemies. "But who else would want to kill Matthew?"

John's grim voice was deceptively steady. "That's what we have to find out, my friend. And soon."

CHAPTER EIGHT

KATHERINE WATCHED Rod Dennison as he manned the bar. When Jessica had hesitantly asked Katherine to consider hiring him, she hadn't had any reason to refuse. And he seemed to be doing a good job.

Sensing Elliott's gaze on her, she looked his way, then began weaving through the tables toward him. She smiled, her eyes filled with feeling.

His hesitation was so brief it was hardly noticeable; then he grinned. "Hey, funny face."

Katherine blinked, wondering where that term had come from. He'd always called her babe. But she didn't feel like quibbling. "Hey, yourself."

Elliott glanced around, looking uncomfortable. "I should probably be checking on something."

She kept her tone amiable. "I don't know. Everything's going smoothly." Unconsciously her gaze strayed back toward Rod.

Elliott's gaze followed hers. "I'm surprised you hired him—" his brow lifted wryly "—considering he's so *well oiled*."

The corners of Katherine's mouth lifted in a rueful grin. "It means a lot to Jessica. And he seems to be a competent bartender."

"Hardly a glowing commendation." His expression grew thoughtful. "Feeling that way and hiring him, anyway...you're a good friend to Jessica."

"It works both ways." Katherine paused, remembering the anxious, even terror-filled moments of single parenthood when she'd realized she couldn't work to bring in the needed income and also stay home to take care of a tiny infant. Her disapproving family had remained distant and cold, not offering any support. "Jessica has never hesitated. From day one she's been there for Dustin and me. I can't do any less."

Elliott was quiet for a moment. "It's an admirable trait. Good friends are undervalued treasures."

It was Katherine's turn to lift her brow. Philosophy from Elliott? She'd have been just as surprised if he'd begun quoting Shakespeare. But she tried not to show it. "You won't get any argument from me. That's why I hired Rod. I don't suppose I have to be charmed by all the people who work for us."

"Does that go for any of the other employees?" Elliott asked.

Puzzled, she tilted her head. "I'm not sure what you mean. You know we handpicked everyone else." Oh, God. Had he forgotten that, too?

"I know that," he said dismissively. "But it doesn't mean you have to love them all."

Frowning, she considered this. "Maybe not. But it's part of why going to work is so much fun. I can't imagine allowing it to become one of those places where people aren't happy. That's one of the best things about being self-employed.''

"Don't like kitchen politics, eh?''

Katherine flushed, realizing she'd mounted her own platform. "I guess I've had more than my share, working for other people. You remember that hotel I worked for?''

He nodded.

"Way too much politics. They had a chain of command that would intimidate the Pentagon, and that just wasn't for me. I wanted to be recognized because I had brains and talent, not because I pandered to whichever manager was the flavor of the day.'' Taking a breath, she released it quickly, ending on a small laugh. "We're so lucky, having our own business. It might have its ups and downs, but…''

"Any downs in particular?'' he asked with apparent increased interest.

"You know, just the usual. When the revenues fluctuate, when we don't get the jobs we really want…''

His gaze was still sharp. "That reminds me. The chamber of commerce wants us to cater their next fund-raiser, and the chairman has an anniversary coming up, as well.''

Katherine's smile broadened. "I *thought* you were drumming up business.''

Elliott halted midmovement. "Oh?''

"Yes. I caught that from across the room.''

"Did you want in on the discussion?"

She shook her head. "You've always been better at bringing in the clients. I just wanted to connect with you. It seems like we haven't had a moment together in—" she smiled and amended her words "—too long. I miss that."

His expression remained unchanging. "Me, too. But I don't want you to take on the bulk of the work."

Impulsively she reached out to take his hand. "I never feel that way. Except for the time it takes me away from you and Dustin, I wouldn't care if I worked from dawn to midnight. We're building more than a business—we're creating a future. Every time I see Dustin making a mud pie, I can't help but wonder if he'll take over the reins one day." She laughed self-consciously. "Or maybe he'll have dreams of his own. Will he grow up to be a doctor, plumber, lawyer, soldier, fireman…"

"Or president?" Elliott suggested.

She laughed again. "Plumber to president? I guess that covers just about everything. Just as long as he's happy—and safe—I won't care."

"You've got time before you need to worry. He's still a little boy."

Katherine swallowed a sudden lump in her throat. "But then, we've only been together a short time, too." Her voice nearly dried up as tears threatened. "Taking life for granted, wishing so many of the less-than-perfect days away—it seems incredibly foolish now. But I never expected this kind of wake-up call.''

''No need to get upset,'' Elliott chided. ''Look how lucky we were.''

Lucky? This kind hand of fate was far more than luck. She glanced toward the bar and caught a glimpse of Jessica as she stood next to Rod. But for that miracle, she could be standing in her friend's shoes, wishing for a husband who would never return home.

SUNSHINE STREAMED through the generous windows in the kitchens of Combined Catering. Light danced off the shiny copper pots and pans hanging from the carousel above the counters. White tile and butter-cup-colored walls continued the cheerful theme.

But Paul wasn't feeling very cheerful.

He intended to goad the employees into revealing how they really felt about working for Katherine. Gritting his teeth and ignoring his misgivings, he watched them work in the kitchen. He had to decide who was going to be the unwitting pawn in his plan.

Approaching Carter, the sous-chef, Paul made sure Katherine was in hearing distance. ''Do you have a new angle for tonight's menu?''

Carter paused. ''New?''

''Yeah. Something a little more…daring than what you've come up with lately.''

Carter's brows drew together. ''Daring?''

"Yep. People have commented that we're not quite as cutting edge as they expect."

"Then maybe you ought to get back to the helm," Carter suggested, his voice rising with each word.

Katherine had inched closer and now she patted Carter's arm. "I don't think Elliott feels quite like taking that on just yet." Her wide eyes implored Carter to calm down.

Paul watched as Carter took a deep breath. "Yeah, okay."

Katherine sighed audibly.

But it wasn't time to let up yet, Paul knew. "No, not okay. What are you going to do about tonight's menu?"

Carter's jaw worked. Then he glanced at Katherine. "I'll work on it."

Paul nodded. "Good." Purposely he walked away, around the corner and out of sight—but not earshot.

Katherine began placating the other man. "I'm sorry, Carter. I'm sure it's just a result of his injury. You know Elliott would never have acted this way when he was…"

"Normal?" Carter supplied.

"I think the accident was really traumatic for him," Katherine continued, her voice cracking. "He hasn't said, but I can tell." She took a deep breath. "It was great of you not to take it personally."

"Right," Carter muttered.

"Really. A lesser man wouldn't have been as understanding. And when Elliott's back to being himself, you'll see. It'll have been worth it for everyone to pull together."

"I wouldn't do this for anyone but you, Katherine. Hell, you know I can take my act somewhere else and not miss a beat. I've had plenty of offers."

"Which is why I appreciate your generosity all the more. Elliott's frozen up about returning to his work—which is probably why he's picking on yours. But without you, I'm not sure how the business would make it. We need you now more than ever."

Carter cleared his throat. "Yeah, well, this has been the best place I've ever worked—or at least it was."

"And it will be again," Katherine assured him. "For me, be patient, and I'll try to keep Elliott out of your way."

"I guess so. But for this much aggravation, I think I deserve more money."

Katherine frowned. "We just gave you a hefty raise."

"Call it battle pay, Katherine."

"You planning on buying a villa on the Riviera?" she asked with a small laugh.

"Does it matter?" he countered, a note of challenge in his voice.

She sighed. "I guess not." Then she hesitated. "But don't tell Elliott about the raise, okay?"

Carter shrugged. "It's your business."

"You can say that again," she muttered.

KATHERINE WASN'T SURE if she should take Elliott to a doctor or just kill him and put him out of his misery. In the past twenty-four hours he'd managed to alienate every single employee. It was as though he was deliberately trying to irritate them.

She had talked herself hoarse, explaining his continuing trauma from the accident, but patience was wearing thin. Alice had confided that if she weren't financially strapped from taking care of her ailing mother, she would have quit on the spot. It had taken enormous persuasion, but everyone had reluctantly agreed to cut Elliott some slack. None of them understood the drastic changes in him.

But neither did she.

Looking at her front door in trepidation, she took a deep breath and eased it open. She stepped inside and stopped. The sound of laughter reached her ears, a deep masculine chuckle and Dustin's childish giggles. But that couldn't be. She purposely hadn't picked up Dustin from Jessica's, knowing she had to talk to Elliott. It wasn't a conversation she wanted her child to overhear.

Hesitantly she took a few more steps and glanced into the living room.

"You're it!" Dustin shouted, waving his toy gun in the air.

Elliott peered from behind the couch. "Hold it, cowboy. That's my horse you're riding."

"Uh-uh!" Then Dustin collapsed into giggles. "I don't got a horse!"

Katherine watched in amazement. Had Elliott returned to being himself? Her heart softened as she watched them.

Elliott walked forward on his hands and knees. "Could be I've got the horse right here." He gestured with his head toward his own back. "You want a ride?"

"Yeah!" Dustin shrieked, running toward Elliott.

"Okay, partner."

With Elliott's help Dustin climbed on his back, and in moments they were "riding" around the room. Elliott still looked awkward in the role, but he was being extraordinarily kind and gentle with her son.

Watching, Katherine sagged against the doorway, pressing one hand against her mouth. Would a confrontation take away the only father figure her son had ever known? Courage faltering, Katherine slipped back into the hall and out of sight. For now she was unable to face that possibility.

JOHN LEWIS, while not usually a particularly cheerful man, looked grim.

Paul swallowed the lump in his throat. Within the parameters of his job, he was accustomed to dealing with the gruesome, the macabre. But it usually wasn't personal. And it didn't come any more personal than his twin's fate.

"Whatever it is, spit it out," Paul said. Not allowing the other man to speak, he continued, "Is it Matthew?" He suppressed the fear. "Do you know something?"

John shook his head. "No, Elliott. The status on that is the same."

Status. It was an efficient realistic term. But now that he was on the other side, it seemed incredibly cold. "Is there something else?"

"Yes. I checked out the child's father."

"Dustin's?" Paul knew who John referred to. Somewhere along the way he had stopped thinking of Dustin as "the child."

John looked at him oddly. "Yes. Apparently the father has been out of the picture since before the child was born."

"Dustin," Paul corrected absently.

"Right." John's gaze sharpened. "No support payments have ever been arranged, nor visitation rights."

"Katherine didn't deny him visitation?" Paul asked, wondering if she had let bitterness come between father and son.

"Apparently not. There are no court records, which indicates there's never been a legal debate about the...Dustin."

"And you're sure you have the right man?"

John nodded. "It's the name listed on the birth

certificate. It appears they were involved until Katherine learned she was pregnant. The relationship ended then.''

Paul didn't need John to spell out the rest. If he nailed Katherine as Matthew's killer, Dustin would be left an orphan.

CHAPTER NINE

PAUL GLANCED CYNICALLY at the outdoor focal point of the Heart to Heart Wedding Chapel. Moonlight reflected off the man-made waterfall, aided by electric uplights that illuminated the rocks and rushing water. Admittedly the designer had been wise to situate the reception area's outdoor dance floor beside the impressive waterfall. Along with the profusion of camellias and gardenias, Chinese lanterns and gas torchères, not to mention enticing music, the place reeked of orchestrated romance.

The wedding reception was winding down, and the remainder of Combined Catering's duties were being ably handled. And Paul had run out of excuses to avoid being with Katherine.

Since she now stood next to him, he was relieved to see that her mind apparently remained on business. She snagged one of the passing cooks.

"Ben, I think we should take down the last carving station," she said.

Ben nodded tiredly. It had been a long evening.

"Oh, and Ben…"

He turned back, attempting to add a smile to his weary expression. "Yes?"

"Great job! Your dim sum was the talk of the reception," Katherine told him enthusiastically, her hands forming double thumbs-up gestures.

Ben's half smile bloomed into a full grin. "Thanks. I tried something a little different."

"Well, it worked! Maybe you can make them again for the big Fairfax reception. We want that buffet to really dazzle."

Ben's grin grew to such proportions it nearly dwarfed his thin face. "Sure, I'll let Carter know you liked them."

She was still smiling when Ben left, whistling as he headed toward the carving station.

"Good employee relations," Paul commented.

"People need to know they're valued."

"I think it worked. Ben looks pleased."

She nodded. "I know too well how it feels to be on the other side of an ungrateful employer." She glanced back at Paul, her voice changing. "It's something I promised myself I would never be."

Paul caught her inflection. "Really?"

"We're lucky to have the luxury of running things as we please. I think that includes treating people well."

Paul grinned, much as he knew Matthew would. "No argument here."

A shadow passed over her face, and he guessed she was debating whether to press further about how he had been treating the employees. But she let the thorny issue drop as she held out one hand. "It looks like everything's under control. Will you dance with me?''

Uneasily Paul accepted her hand, deliberately holding her as far away as possible. They danced to the remainder of the song, and when the music faded away, he stepped back, prepared to drop her hand. ''I guess we'd better get back to work.''

Katherine shook her head. ''Nope. Even Cinderella and her prince get to take a break.''

One of Paul's brows edged upward. ''I've been promoted?''

''You've always been my prince.''

''And I thought I was the court jester.''

She laughed, a soft sound that blended with the waterfall. ''Not so jestery anymore.''

''Oh? Is that a good thing?''

She hesitated. ''I wasn't sure at first...''

''And now?'' he probed, needing to know which twin she preferred.

''You're so strong—'' Katherine lifted her gaze to meet his ''—and that's pretty hard to resist.''

There was a stirring in him that had nothing to do with his mission. Was Katherine truly drawn to him? The music began again and this time he pulled her close. She sighed, a soft sound of pleasure, before sinking against him.

Instantly he remembered the previous afternoon when they'd gone swimming. The incapacitating dryness in his throat when he'd first glimpsed her in a bikini. He could remember every curve, the smooth length of her legs, her alluring cleavage. The image had haunted him in the hours since.

It wasn't a particularly warm night, yet heat was infusing him. Not a slow gentle rise in temperature, but a blaze that erupted.

The music was slow, evocative, provocative.

Paul bent his head, feeling the silky curls of Katherine's hair. Her scent nudged his senses, whispered to his desire.

The press of her breasts against his chest led him to pull her even closer, to fit her hips against his. In response she tightened her hold, lacing her fingers through his hair.

It was madness, Paul knew. But he didn't loosen his hold or relinquish his desire.

They swayed on the dance floor, each movement in unison, each motion bringing them closer—

"Elliott, Katherine." A vaguely familiar male voice intruded.

Paul considered ignoring it, then realized it was probably exactly what he needed. But that didn't curb his resentment.

Reluctantly he pulled away from Katherine. Turning around, he recognized one of the executives he'd met at an event they'd recently catered. "Mr. Dawson, good to see you again."

"I'd like to talk a little business, if you have a moment," Dawson began, no doubt assuming Paul would make the time. "The company's annual meeting is coming up...."

Paul tried not to let his annoyance show. "Of course."

Katherine smiled politely. "I'll leave you gentlemen to talk business while I check on my pastries."

Mr. Dawson smiled back as he patted his stomach. "I'm afraid I can attest to their excellence."

Katherine continued to smile at him, but then shifted her gaze to Paul's. He caught the message there. Clearly she hadn't wanted the interruption, either. Paul's scrutiny remained on her even as Mr. Dawson began to outline the event.

Watching as Katherine made her way across the room, Paul knew he should focus his attention on Dawson. But somehow he couldn't break the connection he and Katherine had made. He'd wanted nothing more than to keep her in his arms, to take her home and— Abruptly his thoughts screeched to a halt. And what? Bed his brother's wife? And in the process forget that she could be responsible for Matthew's death?

His lips drawn in a grim line, Paul wasn't sure which was worse. The knowledge that she could be guilty or the equal knowledge that, for the moment, he hadn't cared.

KATHERINE PUTTERED around the bedroom, glancing every other minute at the doorway. Unable to quench her longing, she tried to soothe her restlessness. Parting the curtains at the window, she stared out into the night, seeing the splash of stars in the ebony sky. Each twinkle seemed to ask why her longing remained unanswered, unfulfilled.

She'd thought surely tonight he would come upstairs, leave the dusty ledgers behind. Hugging her arms against the chill of her thoughts, Katherine turned from the window. She glanced down at the filmy negligee she'd chosen and made up her mind. She couldn't force Elliott to come upstairs, but...

After changing into jeans and an off-the-shoulder cotton sweater, she studied herself critically in the mirror, deciding finally it was a casual but innocently alluring look. She slipped her feet into sandals, took one last look out the window and made a wish on a star. Better than a lucky penny, she told herself, reaching quickly into her jewelry box before she could change her mind.

All but skipping downstairs, she stopped at the French doors to the study and threw them open. "Okay, you. No more shutting yourself in. We have one of the most beautiful beaches in the world practically in our front yard. I don't think we should let it go to waste one more minute."

Elliott looked up at her with drawn brows. "Walk on the beach now?"

"Yes. Right now."

"It's nighttime, in case you haven't noticed."

"One of the best times, in my opinion. There's a full moon—plenty of light to see by." Purposely Katherine lightened her voice and winked at him.

"Besides, it's the perfect time for romance—or smugglers."

"Is this multiple choice?" he asked, looking slightly uneasy.

"If you want it to be," she replied evenly, not showing the sudden prick of hurt. Did he detest the idea of romance with her so much?

"We can't just leave Dustin," he protested.

Katherine sighed. "He's at Jessica's, remember? Just like the other nights we work late, sleeping over with Brian."

"Right, so they can go to Zorak," Elliott replied.

Surprised, she tilted her face in question. "You remembered Zorak?"

"It's not easy to forget," he said, thawing finally. "Dustin's been talking Zorak day and night. I didn't realize the spaceship took off today."

Katherine laughed softly. "Right on schedule. Now come on. Let's not waste another moment of that moonlight."

Elliott hesitated, then smiled. "You're not supposed to encourage me to play hooky."

"Hooky?" she echoed in disbelieving tones. "You've been working at least eighteen hours today."

"If that's what it takes," he replied easily, standing at last.

As Elliott walked from behind the desk, she could only stare at him in renewed surprise. When he talked this way, Katherine felt as if she scarcely knew him. And it was becoming increasingly difficult to ignore the changes.

KATHERINE WAS RIGHT, Paul admitted silently. The beach at night was especially beautiful. And intriguing. The shadows, the moonlight, the rush of the incoming tide. Salt stained the air, as did the odors of seaweed, damp sand and the ever-present hemp. Lights from the piers strung out toward the ocean like pathways to other worlds. Dark mysterious worlds that beckoned.

Paul felt a beckoning of his own. As if in response to his thoughts, Katherine slipped her hand into his. It was warm and small within his own. Even though he'd been cautioning himself ever since their return earlier that evening against a repeat performance, his pulse quickened. They were only holding hands, he told himself with disgust.

Then she brushed against him, her voice rising, and reason fled. "Look, you can see the night fishers!"

He followed the direction of her outstretched arm, but his attention remained fixed on her. Despite the distinctive aromas of the beach, Katherine's scent wafted to him, wriggling its way past his defenses. It was a scent that whispered clean, feminine. Understated yet provocative.

Reining in his thoughts, he walked forward. "We could look for driftwood for centerpieces."

"And treasure."

Paul laughed. "Treasure?"

"Pieces of a shipwreck..."

"And what could we find from a shipwreck?" His tone was skeptical.

"Most anything. That's the wonder of it. The sea harbors a world of secrets. But every so often the ocean releases one, washing something onto the beach. It could be part of a mast from the ship itself. Or a passenger's belongings, maybe gems or colored glass—they're equally precious bits of history."

Surprised, Paul stared at her, seeing that she looked completely serious. "You think the value of gems and colored glass is the same?"

Katherine's smile was wistful, her expression fervent. "Perhaps the glass was part of a young bride's dowry, a bride who never reached her destination, never had her fairy-tale wedding. To her heartbroken groom, that fragment of hope would be priceless."

Paul searched her face. The hopeful romanticism he found in it was difficult to doubt. Shaken by the discovery, his voice was gruff. "You can't count on finding treasure, you know."

Katherine's smile was a thing of beauty. "I know."

They walked along quietly for a few moments. Paul wondered at the rightness of the feeling.

They stopped at a piece of driftwood in their path.

"Too big," Paul said, seeing close up how large it was.

"You're right. And I hate to break up the big pieces."

"Still looking for treasure?" Paul asked gently as he watched her continue to scan the beach.

"Yes, but I also want to find sand dollars," she replied, her hand still in his, her eyes bright with the adventure of the hunt.

"They'd probably be all broken up by the time they washed ashore," he said, hating to always be the pessimist.

"But to find one that's perfect is worth a lifetime of searching," she returned. Then she cupped his jaw. "Just like you, it was worth the wait."

Any appropriate response remained stuck in his throat. It should be something glib, he thought. Glib, however, was beyond his ability at the moment.

But she was bending down, looking at something in the sand. Then she rose, dusting off her hands.

"Nothing good?" His voice was husky.

She shook her head. "Fool's gold. But I'm not taken in by the bright shiny stuff."

Insanely Paul was beginning to wonder if he was. Katherine was as enticing as any bright shiny trinket.

"Let's bury our toes in the sand!" she suggested excitedly, bending to pull off her sandals.

He hesitated.

"Come on, don't be an old poop!"

It was hard to resist her infectious enthusiasm, and he knew Matthew wouldn't have hesitated. Resigned, Paul kicked off his shoes. She grabbed his hand and tugged him to the water's edge, stopping just short of the incoming tide. She stood still as she buried her toes in the sand.

Paul joined her, feeling the cool sand beneath his feet. It didn't take long for the ocean to work its magic, as the waves neared the shore, each lap coming closer. Katherine again slipped her hand in his, swaying toward him. Their bodies connected and the jolt had nothing to do with the water that foamed around his ankles.

Paul turned toward her. He pushed the hair from her face, the curls even wilder in the moist night air. He could feel her tremble beneath his touch. And that vulnerability drew him more than any seductive gesture could.

He pulled Katherine close and her breasts grazed his chest. Beneath the moonlight her violet eyes shone like rare gems, long lush lashes framing them. But it was the emotion in their depths that struck him. Hope, love—and stirring desire. The combination staggered him. Spellbound, he cupped the back of her neck, his hands connecting with a length of silky hair. Then he bent his head and brought his mouth to hers.

Gentleness vanished and heat took its place. Edging her mouth open, Paul felt the sweet sigh of her breath. The sweetness inflamed him, urging further exploration. There was an excitement in her touch that was unlike anything he'd ever experienced.

Even with Susan it had never been like this. Feelings, sharp and poignant, made him pause. Had all that anger been worth it?

Conflicted, Paul slowly drew back, seeing the questions in Katherine's eyes, the flush in her cheeks. He placed two fingers over the hollow of her throat, feeling the rapid pulse, which revealed more than words.

"Elliott?" she asked softly.

"It's me, not you," he responded, unable to transfer his pain to her. "Be patient with me."

Gently she took his hand. "I have the rest of our lives. I can wait." Then she reached into her pocket and withdrew a gold ring. She slipped it on his left hand, her gaze lifting to meet his. "I know how much your wedding band meant to you. It's not as good as having your memory back, but at least I can give you this part of your past."

Speechless, he could only gaze between the caring in her eyes and the ring she'd placed on his finger.

"It's an exact duplicate." Katherine smiled, her fingers easing over the warm burnished gold. "I don't think anyone other than the maker could tell them apart."

His throat closed. If she wasn't what he suspected, if Matthew hadn't survived, she was in for a world of pain. And his actions were multiplying that beyond comprehension. Beyond anything he had ever intended.

"ELLY-UT!" DANNY CALLED, dragging his wagon across the yard toward the deck.

Paul glanced up, a grin creasing his face. The kid was something else. He'd become a virtual shadow. "Over here, champ."

The little wagon filled with boards rattled as Dustin approached. "I gots more lummer," he announced.

"We'll need quite a bit of lumber to finish the job," Paul told him, watching as Dustin earnestly unloaded the small pieces of wood Paul had already cut. He didn't want the kid handling any nails or real tools, and hauling the boards kept him happy.

"How comes there's a hole in the deck?" Dustin asked as he carefully stacked the wood.

"Your mom said a tree limb fell down in the last big storm."

Dustin's small lips pursed in a frown. "Oh, yeah. She wouldn't let me play out here till it was fixed."

"She was afraid you'd get hurt, champ. It's a pretty big hole, big enough to swallow you. We'll have to make sure it's shored up before you start playing on the deck again."

Dustin nodded, digging into his plastic toolbox. "I gots a hammer."

"Good. I can use all the help I can get."

Dustin grinned, a miniature imitation of his mother's sunshine smile. "We gonna fix that hole?"

"Yep."

"Mommy'll be surprised," Dustin told him as he

unloaded more of his play tools. "She didn't think you was ever gonna fix it."

Pausing, Paul stared at him. Procrastination wasn't a good example to set for a child. "Well, I'm going to try to be better about not putting off things."

Dustin screwed his small face into a mask of concentration. "What if you don't like the stuff you have to do?"

"Even more reason to do it right away. It's easy to do the stuff you like, but it builds character to face what you don't like."

"What's char...?"

"Character is what makes a man really a man. It's the part of you that tells you to do the right thing, even if it's not what you want to do, and even if it's easier to do something wrong."

Dustin crunched his face in renewed concentration. "Like when Mommy says the good voice is always inside—you just gotta listen to it?"

Impressed, Paul nodded. "That's right."

Dustin scuffed his feet. "What if you don't listen to the voice?"

Paul studied the boy's face. "Depends. Want to tell me about it?"

Dustin continued to scuff his feet, but finally lifted troubled eyes to meet Paul's. "Brian's got *all* the *Star Wars* guys..."

"And?"

"I wanted one, but Brian wouldn't let me have it…"

"And?" Paul prompted again.

"I took it," Dustin admitted, his voice reduced to a mumble.

"Did you have fun with it?"

Slowly Dustin shook his head. "My tummy hurts when I play with it."

"Do you know why?"

Another shake of the head.

"Sometimes that little voice inside lives in your tummy. And it's trying to get you to listen. Do you know why?"

Dustin's lips trembled. "'Cause taking something's wrong?"

"You got it, champ. Do you know what you have to do now?"

Dustin thought for a moment. "Give it back?"

"Yep. Know what else you have to do?"

Dustin shook his head, tears starting to well.

"You have to tell Brian you're sorry."

The tears began to fall.

Instinctively Paul picked up Dustin and put him on his lap. "Would you like me to help you do that, champ?"

Dustin's sniffles lessened. "Uh-huh." Still his lower lip wobbled.

Paul drew him close. "You made a mistake, Dustin. But that's how we learn to do the right things.

We all make mistakes.'' Paul thought of Matthew. ''I made some bloopers growing up.''

Dustin hiccuped a remaining sob. ''Like what?''

''Like the time I locked my brother in the gardener's shed because a girl we both liked was coming over. Even then he was a charmer, and the girls always liked him better.'' He and Matthew had been twelve at the time, and Paul hadn't thought about the incident in years.

''Did you get in trouble?''

''Sure did. But more importantly I learned it was something I shouldn't have done. And you know what?''

Dustin's head was nestled against Paul's chest in a trusting manner. ''What?''

''My brother forgave me and we were still the best of friends.''

''Like me and Brian?''

''Just like you and Brian. You two are as close as brothers.''

''What's your brother's name?''

''People always called both of us Elliott,'' Paul replied gruffly.

Dustin thought about that for a minute. ''And the other Elly-ut wasn't mad at you?''

''Some. And Brian may not be happy when you tell him at first, and that might make you feel bad. But that's how you learn, too.''

Dustin's face scrunched up again. ''Is that consk-ences?''

Paul studied him for a moment. "Consequences? Yes, that's exactly what they are." Katherine had taught him well.

"Stuff's hard, Elly-ut."

"It sure is, champ. But when you've done the right thing, it'll make you feel good all over. Your tummy won't hurt when you play with Brian, and that little voice inside will be saying happy things."

"I like happy things."

Paul met the boy's trusting unblinking gaze. "Me, too, Dustin. Me, too."

JESSICA'S HOUSE was a place of calm, a port for every emotional storm. A pineapple, the traditional symbol of Southern hospitality, was carved above the front door. Though small, the house had an illusion of spaciousness. Warm splashes of deep lavender and tropical red welcomed visitors into the comfortable sitting area. It was an open-floor plan, with bedrooms tucked off on a side wing.

One wall of the main living area was all windows. Jessica's drafting table stood in a prominent spot, drenched with the favorable light. Beside the table were neat carriers filled with rows and rows of paints, pencils and markers, creating a vivid palette all their own.

Because the children were equally fascinated with the art supplies, Jessica had set up an area just for them, with a miniature carrier generously stocked with appropriate children's markers and paints.

There were two pint-size easels and stools, as well, one for Brian and one for Dustin.

Jessica walked in from the kitchen with a tray. "Iced tea and cookies," she said to Katherine. "I guess it should be something a little more grown-up, but with kids in the house..." She shrugged eloquently. "At least I'm not serving milk!"

"I get enough pastry," Katherine reminded her with a smile. "Give me an Oreo any day." She took one, immediately popping it open to taste the cream filling.

Jessica smiled as she picked up her cup of tea. "I guess we never really get that far from our roots."

Katherine frowned as she reached for another cookie. "You really think so?"

"I wasn't trying to be particularly deep or philosophical," Jessica replied. "Just that we all tend to fall into the ruts we're accustomed to."

"I hope not. I'd like to think I left my own cold roots far behind."

Jessica smiled gently. "As an impartial observer, let me say you most definitely have."

"Impartial? Ha!" Katherine's smile softened. "Glad you're not impartial, actually. But enough of me. How are things going with Rod?"

For the briefest of moments a line appeared between Jessica's brows. It disappeared so quickly Katherine almost wondered if she'd imagined it. "Okay, I guess."

"That doesn't sound like an overwhelming endorsement."

Jessica laughed deprecatingly. "I didn't mean it like that. I guess I was used to so much with Michael..." Her voice trailed off and her eyes brightened suspiciously.

Katherine rose from her chair to sit beside Jessica on the couch. "Has something happened to bring up the memories?"

Jessica's smile was bittersweet. "It doesn't take anything special. Those memories never go away."

"Oh, Jessica!"

"It's not all bad. The pain does fade with time. But remembering how it was then..." She glanced around the room. "It gets lonely, not having someone special to share everything with. You know, the worries—" her smile eclipsed her words "—the silly things. The love."

Katherine trod carefully. "And you don't think Rod could be that special man?"

Jessica's eyes clouded. "I wanted so much for him to be, but now I'm not sure."

"It's early in the relationship," Katherine offered, struggling to remain neutral, since she, too, wasn't certain that Rod was special enough for her friend.

"You're right." Jessica glanced out the oversize windows. "And maybe there's only one true love in a person's life. Perhaps the rest is just surface."

"That's not what you told me," Katherine reminded her gently, "when I met Matthew."

"But you don't think Dustin's father was really a true love, do you?" Jessica asked.

Katherine shrugged. "That's hard to say. I certainly didn't expect Taylor to be as rigid and demanding as my family was. You know that I tried to change to please him. And, of course, he was furious when he found out I was pregnant, even angrier when I refused to have an abortion. Yet, when our relationship began, I thought I loved him. Isn't that all we can go by? What we know at the time?"

Jessica nodded. "I suppose. Do you think I shouldn't compare Rod to Michael? Maybe no one will ever live up to Michael's memory. Maybe I should just accept Rod as he is."

"Maybe." Katherine wavered. It was becoming even more difficult to remain neutral. "I'm not sure a little comparison is wrong. After all, Michael did make you happy. Maybe someone with his same qualities will, too."

Jessica frowned again and chewed on her lower lip. "And you don't think Rod has those qualities?"

"I honestly don't know him well enough to say," Katherine replied truthfully.

"Maybe we need to spend more time together." Jessica's eyes lit up. "As couples, I mean. You and Elliott, Rod and me. But not when Rod's bartending at one of the events for you. That doesn't count. We need to be in an unstructured situation where you and Elliott can get to know him better."

"Sure, we'll set up something soon."

Jessica brightened further. "You told me you don't have anything booked tonight and I know Rod's free. Why don't we go dancing?" She waggled her brows. "You and Elliott can show Rod how happy married life can be."

Surprised, Katherine stared at her friend. Was she already thinking of Rod in those terms? She met Jessica's excited eyes and realized that was exactly what she was thinking. "I didn't know things had become that serious."

Jessica's brightness dimmed slightly. "It hasn't. But with your help…"

Briefly Katherine thought of her own experience with Taylor. Pushing aside the memory, she smiled. "Then I guess we're your matchmakers."

CHAPTER TEN

PAUL HADN'T REALLY THOUGHT much about the resurgence of big-band music. It had been a long time since he'd had the time or inclination to get anywhere near a dance floor. But the newly revitalized Stardust Ballroom was growing on him.

Despite the requisite glittering ball that dominated the high ceiling, the room had a wealth of dusky corners. And the music provided opportunity for contact. Lots of it.

Paul held Katherine in his arms as they whirled to the dreamy notes of the song. No wonder people considered the forties a romantic decade, he decided. Instead of a loud beat that ratcheted the senses, this was a gentler more pervasive intrusion.

Paul tightened his hold on Katherine's waist, but regrettably the song drew to a close. As they hesitantly stepped apart, Katherine's gaze caught his, an incredibly sweet smile curving her lips.

His breath quickened and he stepped toward her again. The pace of the music changed suddenly to a fast swing tune that had the crowd tapping their feet. Paul tried to get his breathing and senses back on track.

"I'm game if you are," he challenged, holding out one hand.

She accepted it with a grin. "You know I am."

Along with the rest of the crowd, they swung, dipped and turned to the magnetic music. Laughing and nearly out of breath when the song ended, they wove a path back to their table.

"I thought the members of a swing band would be about a hundred years old," Katherine observed, glancing at the group whose oldest member couldn't have been more than twenty-three or twenty-four.

"Instead, *we're* the geezers," Paul responded dryly.

Katherine tapped his arm lightly in reproof. "Not that it shows, I hope!"

"On you, not a minute," he responded truthfully. She could have passed for nineteen, he thought, with her wild hair and youthful enthusiasm.

She smiled, her face dimpling prettily.

"You two act like honeymooners," Jessica observed, smiling as she looked at them.

Katherine blushed.

Jessica rolled her eyes. "Okay, I'm convinced." She glanced at her date. "Don't you think so, Rod?"

"Sure," he responded, his gaze flicking over the crowd as it had all evening. It was as if he was searching for something or someone.

Watching him, Katherine felt uncomfortable.

When she'd been single, she'd hated it when a man was with her but still kept checking out the crowd.

Just then, Rod turned to Jessica as though he'd had his attention focused on her the entire time. He leaned forward, moving his fingers through her long blond hair, then kissing her intimately.

Katherine looked away. Luckily Rod chose that moment to ask Jessica to dance.

"Thank goodness," Katherine breathed when they were out of earshot.

Elliott looked at her with interest. "For what?"

"Let's just say I've had enough of Rod for a while."

He glanced toward the departing couple. "Still don't approve of the boyfriend?"

"Not really." Katherine lowered her glass. "Do you?"

Elliott shrugged. "Not my place to say."

She blew out an exasperated breath. "We're not taking an indictment to the grand jury here, just an opinion."

"Okay. Rod doesn't really seem to be her type."

Katherine turned so she could see Rod and Jessica better. "He's tall, muscular, blond." She ticked the items off on her fingers. "Admittedly he's good-looking…" Her voice trailed off as realization struck her.

"What?"

"Rod looks a little like Michael," she said. "Not the strength of character, but the basics. I wonder if in her mind's eye Jessica sees Michael's face when she looks at Rod.''

''Is it that close a resemblance?''

''Not really. But sometimes a person sees what they want to see instead of the truth.''

Elliott angled his head. ''Is that so?''

''You know what I mean. Jessica misses Michael terribly—she's never gotten over losing him. So when she looks at Rod, the edges get a little fuzzy. The whole picture blurs.''

''You think someone can actually do that?'' he asked soberly.

Katherine studied his expression to see if he was teasing, then she relaxed. ''Yes. We all do it some-times. Parents do it when they look at their not-very-well-behaved children and see little angels. Grown children do it when they look at their aging parents and still see them as they were when they were younger, refusing to see how frail they've become. Sometimes we're so desperate to hang on to the fa-miliar that we can no longer see the present—what's real, what isn't. And sometimes we all need the fuzzy edges.''

Paul unexpectedly took her hand. ''We do, huh?''

Warmth flooded her cheeks. ''I think so. I'm sure you've needed some fuzzy edges of your own lately.''

He straightened in his chair. ''Meaning?''

''The world's not always a pretty place, but when

it's completely unfamiliar, I suppose it can be down-right ugly.''

"You're right. It has been difficult.''

She nodded. "I thought so.''

"And it's not easy pretending to know things I don't.'' He looked away, not meeting her glance, afraid she'd spot the pretense in his eyes. "Mostly I hate knowing I'm disappointing you by not recovering my memory any faster.''

Katherine squeezed his hand. "That's not what you should be worrying about! All I care about is you getting well.'' She glanced down at their joined hands. "And I don't want to put pressure on you.'' Hesitantly she met his eyes. "When I talked with Jessica this afternoon, I realized how much she still misses Michael, and...how lucky I am.'' Her lashes drifted closed for a moment. "How very lucky. As long as you're safe, I don't care how long it takes for you to recover your memory.''

Paul pushed even further, knowing he had to. "And if it never completely returns?''

She blanched, swallowing visibly, but she met his eyes. "Then we'll deal with it. If...''

"If?''

Trepidation registered in her eyes along with a trace of fear. "If that's what you want.''

"Why wouldn't I want that?'' he questioned, wondering at this turn in the conversation.

Uncharacteristically she ducked her head. "I wasn't sure you'd still want me.''

Unable to stay the motion, he cupped her chin, gently tipping it upward. To his amazement tears swam in her violet eyes. "Why would you say that?"

She lifted one shoulder in a shrug. "If you don't remember what we shared…"

"I already told you it was me, not you," Paul reminded her, his conscience engaged in full battle.

Jessica and Rod returned to the table just then, both laughing and out of breath as Rod pulled out a chair for her and then sat down, as well.

"Don't tell me you two haven't been back on the dance floor!" Jessica exclaimed.

"We couldn't stand the competition," Paul joked, seeing that Katherine was trying to compose her features and hide the burgeoning tears. "But now that you're not out there showing us up, we could take a stab at it." He stood, holding his hand out to Katherine, offering an escape.

Accepting it, she followed him. Fortunately it was a slow number. Katherine hid her face against his chest. He guided them around the floor, struck by the trust she showed him. As the music continued, she finally lifted her head. "Thanks. I didn't want to ruin Jessica's evening."

He wiped away the last lingering tear that rested just beneath her lower lashes. "And I didn't intend to ruin yours."

She pulled back slightly, meeting his gaze. "You didn't!"

"Well, that's not a smile I put on your face." He pulled her a fraction closer.

She didn't resist, instead sinking against him. The music cooperated, velvety and low, a romantic number that kept them in each other's arms. Their movements slowed until they were swaying together, the rest of the crowd forgotten.

As the music changed subtly, Paul released Katherine just enough to look into her eyes. She reached up, her fingers pausing to stroke the hair that rested on his collar. In the dusky light her unusual eyes resembled smoke. But it was her words that threw him. "How did I get so lucky? To have found someone I love so much?"

Again she nestled against him, saving him from replying, but not shielding him from the thoughts that refused to be stilled.

LOST OPPORTUNITIES. Paul leaned back in the study chair, the darkness of the night shrouding the windows. Like the mounds of paperwork surrounding him, those lost opportunities seemed to mock him. Why hadn't he picked up the phone and talked things out with Matthew? Why had they let a woman—especially someone as shallow as Susan— break them apart?

Paul gripped a pen, his fingers white with the pressure. Would it have killed him to let go of his anger, to take the first step toward reconciliation? His stubborn pride had been at stake, Paul remembered with regret. And what was that pride worth now? Bitterly he realized once more that he had only himself to blame. Matthew had extended the olive branch more than once, but Paul hadn't been able to find it in himself to forgive—and certainly not to forget.

Having taken such a resolute stand as the betrayed brother, Paul had found it difficult to relinquish any of his anger. He'd held on to it with a vengeance. And for what? So he could sit alone in his brother's house and try to learn what had happened to him?

Paul wanted to keep the hope alive, but the voice in his heart had been silent for too long now. He no longer felt the nudges that had been with him since birth, the instincts that spoke from his other half.

Dropping his head into his hands, Paul let some of the agony possess him. From the beginning it had been too dangerous to give in to the emotions. He hadn't wanted them to overpower his reason. Slowly he raised his head, staring beyond the study door. From his vantage point he could see the curve of the stairs, and as easily he could picture the bedroom that lay just above. And in that bedroom…

Tortured, Paul raised his head. While his heart filled with pain over his twin, he still couldn't forget his brother's wife. The invitation in her eyes had been abundantly clear, as was the pain when he'd reluctantly refused the offer.

Tearing his gaze away from the stairway and what it led to, Paul glanced down at the latest computer reports the accounting firm had provided. If there was truth, or even a trail to be discovered, it was here. And despite the dullness in his heart, it was a trail he couldn't abandon. He had failed his brother while he was alive. He wouldn't do it again now.

CHAPTER ELEVEN

JOHN LEWIS LOOKED decidedly uncomfortable as three small children stared at him over the back of the booth. One offered him a bite of a sticky Tootsie Pop, which John declined.

Paul glanced from his friend to the children, enjoying the unlikely scenario. Then he slid into the booth, one brow edging upward as he saw the unlikely ice-cream float John had apparently ordered for him.

"Sorry," John said. "I thought the place would be deserted."

"An ice-cream shop right after school's out for the day?"

"Point taken," John admitted with a reluctant grin. "I haven't been on the ice-cream circuit for a while."

"I wondered why you picked this place," Paul said, glancing around, seeing that all the booths were filled with either mothers and their young children, or high-spirited teenagers.

"Just following procedure. Didn't want to meet in the same place too often," John explained ruefully.

Steeling himself, Paul took a deep breath. "Have you learned anything?"

John's face was shuttered for a moment, then he met his friend's eyes. "Nothing positive, but so far the conclusions aren't good. We haven't located Matthew, but the initial findings point to a nonsurvivor situation."

Matthew, a nonsurvivor. Not in anyone's wildest imagination. Why was it, when one of your own was involved, the terms seemed clinically cruel? Paul searched John's face. "I suspect there's more."

"The chief has scaled back the recovery operation."

Paul winced as the sharp pain he had held at bay surfaced. The fragile hope he'd harbored for his brother's survival crumbled. It was all but official now. "Does that mean your assignment has ended?"

John fiddled with the root beer that had foamed up and pooled at the edge of his glass. "No. The chief's still committed to learning exactly why and how the plane crashed."

Paul looked more closely at his friend. "He's not leaving that to the FAA? It seems to me the official cause of the crash falls under their auspices."

John shifted uncomfortably. "Usually. But you were scheduled to go on that plane with Matthew. In fact, that information was logged on the flight plan and could easily have been leaked. That puts it back in our arena."

Stunned, Paul could only stare at him. Did they think the accident was meant for him?

But John spoke before he could. "Don't go leaping to any conclusions here. There's nothing to point to you as the target yet. But you know the chief—he likes to play it safe. So don't go beating yourself up before we know anything. It won't help your brother—or his family. And you could compromise your investigation."

Paul knew he had to catalog what he'd just been told and not allow himself to feel the emotions the news had caused. At least not yet. "I'm still not sure about Katherine. On one hand I see evidence that makes me believe she has to be connected to the crash. On the other..."

John waited patiently, but Paul didn't conclude the thought. "Any particular evidence?" John prompted.

Paul tried to push aside his pain and collect his thoughts. "A lot of cash was spent—large amounts that aren't accounted for. It could have been foolish overspending. I can tell by the records that the catering company threw some pretty lavish parties to launch the business. Too lavish. And frankly Matthew was never good with money. He liked to make everyone around him happy, regardless of the costs or how proportionate they were to his income. And I understand he withdrew cash that he never recorded, which could explain the missing amounts.

But the accounts show a steady loss that's continuing.''

"When did they start?''

"I can't be certain. I'm trying to run down unrecorded loans or out-of-pocket cash expenses, but I don't have a handle on that yet.''

"Any gaps in the losses? Or have they been consistent?''

Paul paused, remembering. "There have been gaps. In fact, the losses stopped for a while, but they picked up again recently, with the amounts increasing. Which points to Katherine.''

"Sounds like it. Anything else?''

"Matthew's spending tripled when he met Katherine. He must have felt she wanted him to spend that money.''

"So you think she's a gold digger?''

Paul flinched. Baldly stated, it sounded so ugly. "I thought I'd know by now, but I don't have anything definite yet.''

"How's her spending now?'' John asked.

"She hasn't been doing any obvious spending outside of the business.''

"She could be squirreling the money into a hidden account,'' John suggested.

"True,'' Paul admitted, wishing he didn't feel like a traitor for agreeing. "I've wondered if there might be jewelry, too.''

"Have you checked?''

Paul nodded, remembering the day he'd opened

her small jewelry box. There wasn't much inside, only a few simple trinkets that looked more sentimental than valuable. "She has a flashy engagement ring and a few decent pairs of earrings. But I'm guessing that if she has any major stones, they're hidden away in a safe-deposit box."

"Do you want me to check?" John asked.

"Yes, I have to know." Paul wasn't making much progress on his own. Perhaps a third party could learn more.

"We can put a trace on her bank accounts, as well," John said. "Sounds as if you need hard proof at this point."

Paul met his friend's eyes, allowing the professional in him to take over. "Bank accounts, deposit certificates, stocks. I need to match up the losses I've found in the records with corresponding investments."

John's gaze sharpened. "I'll get right on it." He hesitated. "Do you feel you've gotten to know the woman very well?"

Paul nodded cautiously. "Somewhat."

"Do you think she could be what she appears?" John paused. "That is, not considering the missing money."

"But how can I forget that? Death row is lined with men who thought it was motive enough for murder."

"Right." John stabbed at the maraschino cherry

in his melting float. "So you've established a definite pattern from the books?"

Paul shook his head. "It's not a pattern. It's very random, which makes me wonder if that's deliberate, to throw off suspicion. But the end result is the same—the cash is missing."

"Always cash?"

"I'm not certain. It could be in the form of checks that were purposely never recorded. But cash is easiest to steal, hardest to trace."

John frowned. "True. But as co-owner of the company, couldn't she put her hands on the funds at any time?"

"Yes."

"Then why take cash? That's kind of risky—it would be easier for someone to notice. A bundle of cash is a lot more obvious than a check or two."

"True. But checks leave a paper trail."

"That's where I come in, friend." John picked up his glass and tipped it in Paul's direction. "If she's put together a hot drop, we'll find it."

Paul drew in a breath, forcing down the pain. "And we'll be one step closer to knowing what happened to Matthew."

KATHERINE KICKED at the small mound of sand, dislodging a few broken shells. But she wasn't beachcombing today. Even the lure of finding a bit of treasure from an ancient shipwreck didn't interest her. No, she'd come down to the shore for some sense of release.

The wind was a touch cooler than usual, a brisk breeze that carried the scent of the ocean. Breathing deeply, Katherine closed her eyes, flooded by memories. Although her rigid family hadn't been close, once a year they had taken a trip to the shore. That was why she'd bought this home on the beach. It kept her connected to the good times.

"You walk around with your eyes closed like that and you're liable to walk off the end of a pier."

Katherine's eyes flew open at the sound of Elliott's voice. "Oh, I was just thinking," she mumbled, embarrassed. "Besides, we're practically in our own front yard, no piers to worry about."

"Looks more like daydreaming," he countered, falling in step beside her.

"Guilty," she admitted.

"Anything in particular?"

"Just thinking about when my family used to vacation at the beach. It was one of the few times we were almost like a real family."

"Almost?"

"You know they're not a warm group," she responded, then paused. *Did* he know? So much of his memory seemed to be missing.

"That part of my memory's kind of fuzzy."

She laughed humorlessly. "Lucky you. You're not missing much."

"We hitting on something pretty touchy?" he asked.

Meeting his gaze, Katherine saw something smoldering there, and she instantly remembered the feeling of being in his arms the previous night. The memory of their last kiss sprang to mind. The kiss alone had left her limp with desire. But had it affected him that way?

"Katherine?" he urged when she didn't reply.

Shaking her head to clear the thoughts, she replied. "You could say that. I've always wanted the kind of family you and I have made with Dustin. Mine was such a poor example…" Her voice trailed off for a moment. "I just hope I do better by Dustin."

In his eyes, Katherine saw something else, but she couldn't define it. "You're a good mother to Dustin," he said.

"I hope I'm creating something different for him than I had. I want him to know that I'll always love and accept him as he is. The trouble is, I didn't have a good example to follow."

"Some people don't need an example," he said. "Many of the world's leaders come from relatively humble beginnings. They didn't learn by example how to navigate among the power players. They had to find it somewhere deep inside."

She stared at him. He'd done it again—come forth with a profound thought. Where had it come from?

For all of Elliott's wonderful qualities, he wasn't a deep thinker.

"What's wrong?" he asked, studying her, his expression somewhat wary.

She traced the strong lines of his face. "You continue to amaze me."

His expression changed to full wariness. "In what way?"

But she shook her head, unable to articulate her feelings. "You're really something, you know that?"

Confusion clouded his eyes and he didn't reply.

Undaunted, she looped her hands behind his neck and kissed him.

His initial response was cool. Then the heat began. Fire from last evening still smoldered, waiting to be rekindled.

Although his return kiss ignited the same passion, she sensed something else, a bittersweet nearly poignant flavor. She pulled her head back to meet his eyes, and in them she saw an intensity she hadn't expected and couldn't decipher. Pain mixed with longing. Seeing that, Katherine felt an inexplicable pain of her own. Her pulse stuttered for a moment as she wondered what was causing this agony.

"Elliott?"

He didn't reply, only pulled her against his chest in a protective motion, one meant to comfort. But she couldn't decide whom he was protecting. Her— or himself.

As they stood locked together, the ocean continued its eternal pull, sending the tide out to unknown places, the lapping of the waves blending with the cries of gulls. And Katherine trembled as she felt the fingers of unexplained dread reaching toward her. Unable to face the fear, she snuggled against Elliott's chest, hiding from the unknown. Safe for the moment. And refusing to think beyond.

CHAPTER TWELVE

LUSH WHITE SANDS warmed beneath the midday sun. Nearby, straggly wild grass struggled to cover the rising dunes. Katherine sat on a beach towel, facing the water. Dustin cradled her. The pull of the tide increased, bringing the water closer.

Elliott shifted the beach umbrella farther back on the sand, and then picked up the picnic hamper. "Can anyone eat another brownie?"

"I'm stuffed," Katherine moaned, then gave Dustin a rocking hug. "And if this one eats any more, he'll turn into a brownie."

"Aw, Mommy!"

"Dustin—"

"How about if we split a brownie, champ?" Elliott asked him.

Katherine wavered. "I suppose so. But when he's crawling the walls at bedtime, he's all yours."

Elliott shared a conspiratorial wink with Dustin. "I can handle that." Then he sank into the sand beside Katherine. Gleefully Dustin accepted half the brownie.

Katherine regarded the two men in her life as they devoured the brownie and shook her head. She hadn't counted on having them gang up on her. Not that she particularly minded. It was the first time in too long that Elliott had managed a genuine smile.

"Uh-oh!" Dustin hollered as he clambered from her lap. "Look!"

Katherine followed the line of his outstretched arm. "Oh, the tide's coming in."

"My castle!" Dustin shrieked. "My castle!"

"The sand has to go back to the sea," Katherine told him patiently, even though she'd explained tides to him dozens of times.

"Not this time!" Dustin objected.

"You wouldn't want to run out of beach, would you?" Elliott inserted. "If all the sand castles didn't wash back into the water, we wouldn't have enough sand for the beach. And if there wasn't a beach, we couldn't have a house close to the ocean."

"Yeah," Dustin agreed without much enthusiasm.

"Sand castles aren't supposed to last long," Elliott continued. "That's what makes them special. If you woke up every day and saw the beach filled with hundreds of the same sand castles, what would you look forward to? Wouldn't be much point in looking for shells, because the tide wouldn't wash in any new ones. And where would the sea turtles lay their eggs? And that's important because—"

"'Cause turtles is almost ex-stink," Dustin chimed in.

"Extinct, sweetie," Katherine corrected gently as

she enjoyed the interchange between her husband and son.

"Exactly." Elliott agreed. "Besides, if you want to create something that will last a long time, there are other ways to do it."

"Like what?" Dustin demanded.

Elliott smiled. "All kinds of things. You can build a tree house…"

"Mommy won't let me use nails," Dustin complained.

"If you want to build a tree house, I can handle the nails," Elliott assured him. "But there are other things that can last that long." His eyes took on a faraway expression. "My brother and I made a time capsule and buried it in our backyard."

"What's that?" Dustin asked, climbing into Elliott's lap.

"A time capsule is a collection of things that you care about. Then, when you're older, you can dig it up and see what was important to you when you buried the capsule."

"What was in yours?"

Again that faraway look came into Elliott's eyes. "All kinds of things, things that meant something to us. We put in my brother's favorite comic book, a robin's egg that we were convinced was really a dinosaur egg, a crystal doorknob that we used to believe would turn into a giant diamond if we kept it buried long enough." He laughed, but the sound faded away. "And a picture of our family so we would always remember how it felt to be together."

"Can I make one?" Dustin asked excitedly. "I'll find some *real* dinestore eggs."

Elliott ruffled his hair. "Maybe so. And if not, I'm sure you can find some other treasures."

"Probably right here on the beach," Katherine suggested, her gaze meeting Elliott's. "I know my treasures are within arm's reach right now."

"Sand dollars!" Dustin exclaimed, not catching her deeper meaning.

But his enthusiasm made her smile. "If we're lucky. Now you'll have to decide where to bury your time capsule."

Dustin scrunched up his face. "Do I hafta tell?"

She blinked in surprise. "I suppose not."

Forgetting about his sand castle, Dustin scampered away. He turned back briefly and yelled, "Gonna get shells!"

"I didn't think he was old enough to want secrets," she murmured. "They grow up so fast."

"Hey, don't go all mushy. He's three, not thirty. Your baby's not quite ready to leave home."

"Very funny," she retorted, shaken out of her musing. "But he is growing up."

"That's inevitable."

"Unfortunately. I don't suppose I could freeze-frame him at this age."

"And miss all the fun of watching him grow

older? What about his first day of school? His first two-wheeler? The prom? Graduation?''

Katherine felt the catch of emotion that started somewhere in her throat and settled in her heart. ''You're such a wonderful father to Dustin. We're so lucky to have you.''

A cloud drifted over his expression, but Katherine refused to pull back. Instead, she fitted herself into his arms, her back against his chest, for the first time not wishing for things to be as they had been.

ALONE IN THE STUDY, Paul emptied the contents of Katherine's safe-deposit box. He had met John briefly to take possession of the small packet, but he hadn't wanted to examine the contents with an audience. For this he needed privacy. Because that box had also belonged to his brother.

The first item to tumble out was a small plastic box containing a lock of baby hair and Dustin's birth ID bracelet. Turning the innocent items over in his hands, he wondered at the woman who considered these mementos so important that she placed them in a safe-deposit box.

Seeing a glint of gold, Paul reached for the item, his stomach lurching as he wondered if this was the cache of jewelry Katherine was hiding. Pulling the fine serpentine chain toward him, he saw that it was a simple gold locket. Clearly its value was primarily sentimental, since such an item wasn't that expensive.

He put the locket down, then glanced at it again. Picking it up, he found the tiny fastening that held the two sides together. Unable to squelch his curiosity, Paul opened the locket. The photo inside made him catch his breath. Matthew's grin jumped from the picture, almost as electric in the photo as in person. He reached out a finger to touch the familiar features, feeling the silence in his heart. Closing his eyes, he allowed the reality to settle. Matthew wouldn't be coming home.

The shadows in the room lengthened as Paul stared at the locket, remembering all the good, all the bad, the unique bond of twin life they'd shared. Bending his head to rest his face in his hands, Paul felt the hot splash of tears. Tears he hadn't allowed before. The anguish of loss coupled with regret. Why hadn't he repaired their break earlier? How could he have allowed pride to sever something so important?

He didn't know how much time had passed when he finally lifted his head. The lump of emotion in his throat told him he had been paralyzed by the grief for some time.

Forcing himself back to the task at hand, he reached into the small pile, his hand stilling suddenly. A pocketknife glinted in the lamplight. The pocketknife he had given Matthew for their sixteenth birthday, his brother's initials crudely carved on the stock. Swallowing hard, Paul picked it up and turned it over in his hands. Laughing carefree Mat-

thew had apparently treasured the gift enough to
lock it safely away. Until that moment Paul
wouldn't have believed that Matthew cared enough
about anything to lock it away. Regret stabbed
again. Closing his eyes, Paul sent a silent message
to his twin, one of remorse and promise.

That promise forced him to examine the remaining contents. But there was remarkably little to see.
Dustin's birth certificate, Matthew and Katherine's
wedding certificate and a few small savings bonds
in Dustin's name. Hardly an arsenal of accumulated
wealth. Certainly not enough to kill for. In fact, it
was a sparse collection by any comparison. No jewels, stocks or cash.

So where did that leave him? Did he believe that
this evidence, combined with Katherine's apparent
sincerity, proved her innocence? Slowly he reached
for the locket, his fingers closing around the warm
gold. Until he knew for sure, he couldn't assume
anything. For Matthew's sake he had to continue.

As the night deepened, Paul sat alone, one hand
filled with the locket, the other with the pocketknife,
while his heart filled with grief.

NEARLY TWO WEEKS had passed since Katherine had
glimpsed the agony in Elliott's eyes. Since then he
hadn't turned to her for comfort again. Yet she
sensed something was very wrong. On the few oc-
casions his expression was unguarded, she had seen
the pain. He had been remarkably tender with Dus-

tin, almost as if being with the little boy gave him something he needed.

And that made Katherine want to reach out to Elliott even more. But so far she had failed. He was so quiet. Unnaturally quiet. Of course, he had been more reserved than usual since the accident, but this was different and far more pronounced. Yet he refused to take a break from work. And Katherine worried that if he continued on this way it would make his memory loss worse.

Luckily tonight's function was a small one—an intimate wedding reception held at Rose Plantation, a renovated antebellum mansion. Katherine had always admired the place. It was small by plantation standards; but much like gifts, sometimes the best ones come in small packages.

Aged brick, faded to a dusty pink from years in the hot summer sun, soared upward with sweeping grace. Ivory columns flanked the portico that opened into a marble entryway. Leaded windows sparkled beneath the light of the chandelier, its sconces fashioned in the shape of calla lilies. Katherine always thought the place reeked of history and romance. It even had a touch of mystery.

The reception had wound down and only a few couples remained, swaying to the gentle music. They seemed reluctant to relinquish the magic of the night. Glancing at Elliott, Katherine was forced to agree with them.

Unexpectedly he raised his head, his gaze locking

on hers. Hope stirred when he didn't look away. Approaching him, she felt her heartbeat quicken when his eyes darkened. Emboldened, she quickened her stride. As she reached him, she held out her hand and asked softly, "Will you dance with me?"

His eyes probed hers, instantly reminding her of their repressed desire, the tension that was reaching unbearable proportions. Without replying, Elliott drew her close. It was an intimate pose, one that stunned the senses, then sent them into a dizzying acceleration.

The music resembled the Carolina night, deep and slow. The languid beat encouraged them to linger in one spot, their movements little more than joint swaying, an undulation that threatened to consume them both. It was a motion that tantalized, an enticement that crept beneath the skin, whispered to the blood.

Ocean breezes that stirred the hot air did nothing to lessen their building heat. It was a heat that simmered with awakened and unfulfilled passion. Like the overpowering scent of sun-drenched magnolias, the yearning thrummed between them, sweet and hot.

Music forgotten, Katherine twined her fingers through Elliott's hair. She wondered that her pulse didn't fly through her heated skin when his lips whispered against her neck. Trembling beneath his touch, she was overwhelmed by the unfamiliar feelings and the intensity of her reaction.

Throwing back her head, Katherine glimpsed the matching passion in Elliott's eyes. The anticipation was almost a visible thing that lingered in the humid currents of the night and searched for a passage of its own.

Beyond their thundering hearts, they could hear the notes fading away as the music ended. They didn't, couldn't, part immediately. Instead, Elliott shifted his hand to cup the back of her neck, his eyes never leaving hers.

Only when the remaining couples started to shuffle past did they move. And then only with excruciating reluctance, their hands still linked.

For the first time since they'd begun the business, Katherine left the cleaning and packing to the other employees without explanation. Once she would have said they couldn't simply walk away and give in to the urges possessing them. But the heat hadn't lessened; instead it built, blinding her to all else.

For the moment she didn't care if her actions were uncharacteristic. Her pulse still hadn't settled into a normal pattern. And glancing at Elliott, she doubted it soon would.

PAUL GLANCED at the open study door, then up the curving staircase. The floor plan was imprinted in his mind and he knew precisely how close the bedroom was, how few steps it would take to reach Katherine.

He could picture her easily, remembering vividly how she'd stood on the bottom riser when they'd returned home earlier that evening. Katherine had begun to climb the stairs when she paused, turned and asked if he would be coming upstairs soon. Her meaning had been clear, his reply more muddled. He knew they were close to crossing a line, one Katherine wouldn't be able to forgive once she learned the truth. His body ached with frustration; his emotions were in a matching state.

Suddenly he heard a cry. Concerned about Dustin, he ran up the stairs. But when he reached the toddler's room, he saw Katherine bent over her son, rubbing his back and murmuring in soothing tones. The night-light cast a soft glow over them both. Knowing Dustin was all right, he could have stepped away. But, spellbound by the touching scene, he didn't move.

Within a short time Dustin drifted back to sleep and Katherine eased off the bed. Her eyes widened with surprise when she saw him leaning against the doorjamb. He read the uncertainty coupled with longing in her expression. The combination was impossible to resist.

Deliberately Paul straightened and stepped closer. She moved closer, too, until there was scarcely a foot between them and a desperate need to eliminate that space as well.

He pulled her from the room.

Awareness shot through the air with the rapidity of an attacking cheetah. And like animals in the wild, their senses were on full alert. Even the air around them seemed to change, charged with the flow of accelerated adrenaline.

Mouths met and fused, sealing a fate that seemed predestined from the start. And suddenly they were in their bedroom, alone. No distractions, no excuses. No barriers.

Paul kicked the door shut as they clung together, hands and mouths moving in frenzied anticipation. He considered the consequences, then shrugged them aside. He couldn't have walked away if the room had burst into flames.

Groaning with need, Paul wound his fingers through her silky hair as he explored her mouth, tasting the sweetness she offered.

Clothes fell away, ripped off greedily as desire overtook caution. Paul couldn't still a gasp of admiration when her honey-colored flesh was revealed.

Then they were on the bed, the mattress dipping beneath their coupled weight. Paul thought again of the consequences, but only for a moment. He desperately needed an affirmation of life, in the face of his brother's death.

Katherine's touch was a balm that inflamed. With each movement, each caress, the fire that had been smoldering leaped higher. His mouth found hers again, feeling the sweet sigh of arousal, the exploration he never wanted to stop. His hands took a reverent journey over her body. A journey he was anxious to begin, yet wanted to prolong. He reveled when she shuddered, then sighed her growing desire.

Her skin sang like silk, her body an enticement he couldn't get enough of. At the same time her hands traveled over his body, each touch coaxing the embers beyond endurance, threatening an inferno.

But it was an inferno he gladly embraced. A pivotal moment that spun out of control, beyond desire, beyond anything he expected.

Then she began to tremble beneath his touch, a quivering that shot straight to his heart. Protectively he cupped her face in his hands, his eyes meeting the violet jewels of her gaze. The moment lingered, suspended in a dimension only lovers share.

She grasped his shoulders, then his neck, urging him closer. His head sank to the soft flesh of her throat, his mouth seeking and finding her pulse, then traveling downward.

He heard her gasp as his mouth encircled one nipple, then felt her arch from the bed, her hands fisting. Still, the desire built and the journey of discovery continued.

Katherine felt her body shattering, the passion like none she'd ever experienced. Eagerly she accepted each touch, each caress so electric it rocked her soul.

Gone was the playful lover she remembered. In his place was an intensely passionate lover who stole her breath. Every movement made her hunger for more, creating an appetite she hadn't known existed. An appetite he was satisfying in ways she'd never imagined.

It was magic, it was unstoppable. The more he gave, the more she craved—and still the feelings built.

She whispered inarticulate fragments, words urging, seeking. In response he sank deep inside her. Instead of stilling her cries, she groaned with a new pleasure, a pleasure so unexpected, she buried her gasp against his throat.

Then his lips found hers again. He plied them with a tenderness equally unexpected. An explosion of joy shattered her heart, eclipsed her wonderment. And the explosions had only begun…

MOONLIGHT PLAYED over the room, a sonata of silver shadows. Paul cradled Katherine in his arms, her dark hair flung like a silken banner over the ivory sheets. Her breasts, which he now knew intimately, were pressed against his chest. His heartbeat remained aligned with hers, and one of his hands rested on the valley of her waist, sliding occasionally over the slope of her hip.

He had needed the affirmation, expected the arousal, but nothing had prepared him for the tenderness. It was etched in his mind like a precious carving so fragile it could easily crumble. Where had this come from? What had taken them to such unexpected places?

Katherine's hand curled trustingly yet protectively at his throat. Lifting her head slightly, she kissed the underside of his jaw.

How could softness send such an intense jolt? he wondered. Had the universe suddenly tilted off center? Or only his own world?

Katherine's lips inched close to his ear as she whispered, "I love you."

And Paul knew it wasn't only his world that had careened off center. It was also the one he had drawn Katherine into—a make-believe world she didn't yet know she'd entered.

CHAPTER THIRTEEN

THE SUNSHINE SEEMED brighter, more vibrant than ever before, Katherine realized as she walked on the beach. It was as though God had dipped the world in new colors, dazzling in their freshness. Smiling with that thought, she waved when she spotted Jessica approaching.

"Hey," Jessica greeted her. "You look like the proverbial cat who swallowed the canary. What's up?"

"Everything!" Katherine replied, unable to squelch her grin.

"Uh-huh," Jessica said, linking arms with her.

Katherine instantly wished that Jessica had someone as wonderful as Elliott in her life. She deserved the same sort of happiness.

"I'm guessing things are better with Elliott?" Jessica said.

"Much." Katherine's voice softened in memory. "It was as though I truly knew him for the first time. I'm not sure how a person can change so much from an accident, but I'm much more in love with him now than before. He seems to have a whole new dimension, one I never saw before, never imagined he possessed. There's depth, excitement..." Her voice trailed off and she glanced self-consciously at her friend. "I guess I sound pretty goopy, don't I?"

"You sure do." Jessica nudged her. "And I'm deliriously happy for you. I know how worried you've been. It sounds as if you both just needed time to rediscover each other."

"I guess so," Katherine replied, remembering the wonder. "But it's more than that. It's almost like he's a different person, one I've fallen deeply in love with. Sometimes I miss his irreverent endless teasing, but..."

"Now he's a man you also admire," Jessica supplied, her wise eyes filled with a special brand of insight, an insight that had proved priceless throughout their friendship.

"You're right." Katherine smiled, realizing how true it was. "I hadn't put a name to the quality, but it is admiration. He has such incredible strength now."

"Before his accident he was the embodiment of your wish for someone who could take you away from the rigidity of your upbringing. But we all need structure and someone to lean on, Katie. And it should be your partner in life."

Katherine realized immediately what Jessica left unsaid. Up to this point she had always turned to Jessica for that support. "Don't ever discount the value of our friendship. I will always need that."

Jessica blinked, her eyes suspiciously bright. "I

know. I never plan to let you forget it, either. But this is what the best of marriage is. It's what I had with Michael. Even though you were my dearest friend, Michael provided the anchor in my life. And when he was gone, I hung on to you for dear life.''

Katherine hugged her friend, feeling the sting of her own tears. ''And I'll always be there for you, Jess. The only thing that could make me happier than I already am today is knowing you have that special love again—'' she paused, hoping she could choose the right words ''—with the right man, one who deserves you. You're pretty special, you know.''

Jessica's laugh was slightly choked. ''We've got a good mutual-admiration society going on here, friend.''

But Katherine couldn't laugh the seriousness away. ''I'm right, you know. The man you choose will be very lucky.''

Jessica ducked her head for a moment. ''Perhaps we only have one chance for that truly special love. Maybe nothing else measures up to those expectations again.''

Katherine shook her head. ''I've been given two chances. Although both have been with Elliott, he's not the same man he was before. And I believe you have that chance, too.'' Her voice softened. ''I hope you believe that, Jess.''

Jessica's voice was wobbly. ''How could I not with you as my cheering section?''

Relieved, Katherine chuckled. "Keep that thought. You know I'll be relentlessly reminding you."

"I shudder to think of the consequences," Jessica replied, a smile breaking through the mixed emotions in her expression.

"That's better. We still have to walk our three miles, and at this rate preschool will be over and the boys will be thumbing a ride home before we get there."

Jessica's laugh mingled with the cries of dive-bombing seagulls.

Glancing at her friend, Katherine issued a silent prayer, hoping that Jessica would know the same happiness she'd found. That Jessie, too, could trust the man she loved.

PAUL WANDERED THROUGH the silent kitchens of the catering company. Though it was midafternoon, most of the staff had left and the vans were filled with the food for the afternoon's event. He paused by Katherine's station. As usual her equipment was immaculate and orderly.

Only a short time ago, she had been designing one of her delectable creations, a few dark curls escaping her chef's hat to rest softly against her forehead. She'd caught him watching and her returning smile had sent his emotions into overdrive. Even now, his gut clenched with the desire that shone in her eyes. But it was more than just desire. It was something purer, something he feared to name.

In his zeal first to avenge Matthew, then to feel the affirmation of life, he had shamelessly played with Katherine's emotions. And unlike broken toys, he could neither repair nor replace those feelings once she knew the truth.

It was time to end the farce, he realized. Time to walk away, to deliver the painful truth and let Katherine begin the healing process.

His heart contracted at the realization she would never want to see him again. The deception would cut too deeply. And that pain would be coupled with the worse pain of losing Matthew. Paul knew firsthand how that would feel. That agony hadn't left him; instead, it was a constant companion, a reminder of why he was in Katherine's life.

His cell phone rang suddenly, breaking into his thoughts.

"Elliott," he answered curtly.

He listened to John's voice and agreed to meet him. The signal in his heart told him the purpose of that meeting. Shutting off the phone, his gaze went again to Katherine's station, and his heart bade her a silent goodbye.

"I'M REALLY SORRY," John repeated, compassion filling his expression and voice.

Paul couldn't speak immediately, his hand still stroking the incredibly cold box that held his brother's remains. His voice was low, gruff with un-shed tears. "There's no doubt?"

John shook his head. "Dental records confirm the identity."

"I already knew," Paul admitted, even though he'd wished for a miracle. Remorse for what could and should have been struck him with a force so strong he gripped the edge of the table for support. "It's as though we shared a heart. I knew when his half stilled. I kept hoping I was wrong." Slowly he lifted his head. "But deep down I knew."

John nodded, not questioning that certainty.

"Just before you phoned, I realized it was time to call it quits," Paul went on. "Time to tell Katherine the truth."

"You don't want to continue the investigation?" John asked in surprise.

Frowning, Paul tore his gaze from the box and looked at his friend. "You think I should?"

"You've come this far, and we're close to learning everything. Why stop?"

Paul remembered Katherine's warmth and softness. "I'm not sure exactly what it would accomplish now."

"The same thing it would have accomplished before you knew Matthew's fate." John paused, watching his friend. "He deserves this one last thing—the truth."

Paul met his friend's gaze. "But does Katherine?"

"We won't know that unless you finish what you started." John hesitated, then took a deep breath. "And with you still portraying Matthew, your own safety won't be compromised."

"My safety?" Paul felt the crack in his heart deepen, the pain intensify. "Do you mean that—"

"We don't know whether you were the intended target, and we won't unless you continue the role you're playing."

Paul wondered if the pain would knock him flat. If Matthew had been killed in his place, he wasn't certain he could ever forgive himself. And if that had happened, in addition to being responsible for his brother's death, he had also ruined Katherine's and Dustin's lives. Swallowing past the grief, he found his voice. "I'll do whatever it takes."

John nodded.

Kneeling beside his brother's remains, Paul made a silent vow. He knew he would keep that vow, even if it meant sacrificing the woman who had ensnared both Elliotts.

DUSTIN'S YOUNG VOICE was the only one Katherine could hear clearly. The rumble that was Elliott's voice was so low, she couldn't decipher the words. Although she stood nearby in the kitchen, putting away the dishes from their late dinner, she felt oddly distanced from her husband and son.

Elliott had been quiet, not even bothering to taste the fresh salmon she'd prepared for dinner, finally pushing away the full plate. And the few times she'd glimpsed his unguarded expression, his eyes looked bleak. She'd thought that after what they'd shared, he was on the road to recovery. Now she wasn't so certain.

And he'd disappeared again that day. She and the staff had set up for a relatively small birthday party, but Elliott hadn't arrived until they were already cleaning up and packing. Luckily it was a low-profile event, which had been handled quickly and easily. Still, she'd wondered where he'd been, but he hadn't offered an explanation.

He seemed content to play with Dustin. As she stepped into the den, Katherine paused, watching them. Dustin had climbed into Elliott's lap, and his eyelids were drooping. Elliott continued stroking his hair. The pain was back on his face, a tortured look that tore at Katherine's heart.

Quietly she approached and sat on the arm of the chair. "I think he's asleep."

Elliott didn't respond right away. Reluctantly he dropped the hand that had been stroking Dustin's hair. "I suppose he is."

Still he didn't move.

Katherine swallowed the fear in her throat, wishing she knew what was causing Elliott such pain. "We don't have to take him upstairs right away."

Elliott nodded.

Katherine gently took his hand, silently offering her strength. She couldn't guess what had disturbed him so, but she knew he needed comforting. Gently she rested her head against his shoulder. He stiffened momentarily, then one arm reached out to encircle her.

Soft moonlight came through the tall open windows. For now, Katherine knew she could ask no questions, only offer comfort. It was no less than he would do for her.

PAUL AND JOHN strolled together along the beach. They both looked like mismatched crosses between natives and tourists. Their tans were darkening, but the clothes weren't quite as casual.

"Any more news on the crash?" Paul asked.

John shook his head. The investigation was still pressing on.

They fell silent as they passed a young couple. Once out of hearing distance, John spoke. "But we have a line on the insurance policy."

Swallowing, Paul prepared himself for the worst. "Yes?"

"The policy you found is active, the beneficiary unchanged."

Paul tried to disregard the disappointment, but it flared sharply. "Oh."

"But we also found a second policy from the same company," John revealed. "It's a matching policy on Katherine with Matthew as beneficiary. There's another smaller policy on her, as well, benefiting her son."

Brows drawn together, Paul stared at his friend. "Matthew and Katherine had identical policies?"

"Yes. Their agent reports that they bought the policies to safeguard against the business collapsing in the event one of them died. It's standard practice in small companies and partnerships."

"Then why haven't I found Katherine's policy?" Paul asked.

"The agent still has it. They hadn't returned it because they were waiting for the report on her physical. It was delayed by her doctor's office. And as the agent explained, their process isn't particularly speedy." John shrugged. "You know how insurance companies are—they move at the speed of dirt. Even though you haven't seen the actual document, it's very much in effect."

Paul shook his head, wishing he could clear his thoughts as easily. "If his death wasn't for the insurance money..."

"Wilkinson still insists it's sabotage," John replied. "At the very least, it wasn't simple mechanical failure. But the agency isn't ready to adopt even that stance just yet. You're too valuable. We're still working on the cause of the fire at Katherine's first business—the results of that investigation should tell us a lot more. Meanwhile, orders are to keep things at the status quo."

Paul couldn't disguise the bleakness in his voice. "I wish it were that easy."

John clapped a hand on his friend's shoulder. "No one's suggesting it is."

Lifting his head, Paul stared out at the ocean. "What would you do in my place?"

"Hope like hell that Katherine is what she appears to be. But for your brother's sake, not drop the investigation until knowing that for certain."

Paul thought of Katherine's sensitivity while not even understanding why he had withdrawn from her. She offered silent comfort and strength, and greedily he'd accepted both. He couldn't help wondering what would happen when she needed those same things—when she learned Matthew's true fate.

Gazing at the endless stretch of water, Paul knew that both her pain and his own would be multiplied by this deception. And even worse, he knew he could not relinquish it.

CHAPTER FOURTEEN

THE NIGHT AIR was filled with a humid, sensuous ripeness that existed only in the South, and only by the dark ocean waters. The languid feeling was so tangible, it seemed to Katherine that she could reach out and touch it.

She lit another candle, a fat jasmine pillar. It joined the proliferation of candles of all sizes, shapes and colors. Some had a fragrance, and others simply oozed the odor of tallow and burning wick. But all cast shadows around the room.

Their light played over the walls, the huge free-standing antique armoire, the crystal vase of roses that pouted in full bloom and the fresh sheets on the bed. Coupled with beams of moonlight that pushed insistently past delicate lace curtains, shadows created shapes only the imagination could decipher.

Katherine studied her reflection in the cheval glass mirror that stood in the corner of the room, uncertainly touching the daring silk confection she wore. It was by far the most sinfully luxurious negligee she'd ever owned.

She desperately wanted to help Elliott, to remove the bleakness in his expression, to see his tender smile once more. Closing her eyes, she remembered that his smile had never been tender before the accident. Now she desperately hoped it could be tender again.

Hearing a rustle directly behind her, Katherine opened her eyes and met Elliott's eyes in the mirror. As she watched, he reached for the clasp that held her hair in place. Unfastening the clip, he watched with her as the wild curls swept over her shoulders. Then his hands wove through the thick mass, the movement simultaneously alerting and lulling her senses, and came to rest on her temples.

She stood motionless as his eyes held hers in the reflection, his hands skimming over her body. He paused with his hands on the delicate straps of her gown. As he slipped the first one down, his lips kissed the spot where the narrow strap had lain. Then the second strap fell, the thrust of her breasts the only barrier holding the delicate fabric in place.

Katherine's breath caught and her blood heated. She fancied seeing the leaping pulse at her throat when he pushed aside her hair, his teeth gently nipping her neck.

Then their eyes met again in the mirror. A languidness that matched the night possessed her limbs. With excruciating slowness he put his hands on the fabric that curved above her breasts. With equal deliberation he pulled the gown free of its last barrier. It fell, pooling at her feet.

She didn't move, and still their gazes connected.

A connection that defied anything she had ever experienced. And with it she felt a desire so intense she almost begged for his touch to continue. But the words wouldn't come. And the heat in his eyes told her to rush.

Still watching, she gasped as he finally touched her naked flesh. Exerting the fiercest of claims, his fingers carved a torturous path over her skin, every nerve ending alive and screaming for more. But he prolonged each movement, building the anticipation to a frenzied pitch.

Trembling beneath the onslaught, her eyelids flickered closed. When she opened them again, she felt amazement as she saw their images in the mirror. His tanned hands were a stark contrast against her pale skin. He wore only a loosely belted robe and she could feel his hardness, an insistent reminder of what they had shared. Then his hands encircled her breasts, each nipple hardening in response. Her body grew taut as the sensations mounted.

His hands drifted down toward her waist, caressing the slope of her hips. Then he paused, waiting until their eyes met again in the mirror. And she realized she had never dreamed of passion this intense. As his hands searched for and opened her up to him, she also knew she'd never dreamed of such fulfillment.

When he finally turned her toward him, she was limp with sensation. He picked her up and carried her to the bed. His robe fell open and impatiently she tugged it away. She needed to feel his hard flesh against her own. Steel and satin. Hard and soft, male and female.

A primitive call beckoned to her, one that made her lock her legs around his back and whisper in his ear, "I want you inside me. I need you. All of you."

The thrust made her gasp, the urgency heating already inflamed blood. She sensed desperation in his passion and wondered briefly which incited the other. But the thought fled as he carried them both to a shattering climax. Feeling him deep inside, she only knew that for the first time in her life she felt complete, and that without him she never would again.

IN THE QUIET AFTERMATH Paul stared at the drifting shadows on the wall. His mind was a blur of conflicting memories and emotions. The loss of his brother had fractured his heart. And, impossibly, he felt Katherine creeping into the fissure that loss had left.

Making love to her was an incredible experience. Her capacity for giving astounded him. He had expected his grief to overshadow all else. But somehow she had taken that on, as well, when she accepted him.

After he and Matthew had fought over Susan, Paul had decided he was meant for a solitary life. Love was for family men, van-driving nine-to-fivers.

He didn't fit into that picture. His wasn't a career that dovetailed with a cozy nest, PTA meetings and neighborhood barbecues. And he knew that was what Katherine wanted. But then, once she discovered his deception, she would no longer want him. End of problem.

His heart couldn't accept that answer. Just as he'd known Matthew was gone forever, he knew the investigation would clear Katherine. And when it did, he would have to confess the truth. He could imagine the betrayal that would flash in her incredible eyes, the hurt that would quiver from deep inside. And again he would be the outsider. But for now, just for now, he could pretend that wasn't going to happen. At least not yet.

KATHERINE AND JESSICA watched Elliott as he helped Dustin and Brian "launch" their cardboard rocket to Zorak.

"He's so patient with them," Jessica commented. "I don't think I've ever seen him devote so much time to the boys."

"He's always been good with Dustin, but since his accident he's brought a new dimension to their relationship," Katherine said. "He's very different in so many ways."

"Still?"

Katherine nodded. "It's not just a few things. It's everything. It's as though he came back a changed man, a completely different person."

"In a good way?" Jessica asked.

"He has a strength that allows him to have more depth, yet also allows him to be flexible."

"So your fears about him becoming rigid were unfounded?"

"Yes, Miss Know-it-all," Katherine replied, her teasing smile fond. "And in this case I'll gladly admit you were right. In fact, I'm ecstatic you were right."

Jessica dusted her hands together. "Then my work here is done."

"Not by a long shot. We still have your romance to get off the ground." As yet Katherine wasn't sure what she thought of Rod, but knew that, as a friend, it wasn't her place to judge, but to support.

Jessica frowned. "Not too much on that front, I'm afraid. I think I may have attributed qualities to Rod he doesn't really have."

"Oh?"

Jessica looked at her somberly, her expression wistful. "I think I wanted so badly to find another man as special as Michael that I've been grasping at straws."

"Does that mean you won't be seeing Rod anymore?"

Jessica shrugged. "I imagine we'll still date. It's nice having an escort who isn't eighty years old and dragging along his oxygen tank, but that's probably about all that's going to come from this relationship."

"As long as your eyes are wide open, you'll be okay. And you can keep your gaze in shape by watching for Mr. Right," Katherine suggested.

"I don't think he exists," Jessica replied glumly. "I met a nice guy at the coffee shop this morning, but of course he's just passing through town."

"Maybe he'll be back."

"Maybe, but I'm not counting on it." Jessica sighed mightily. "The good ones are either taken or just passing through."

"And you're sure he's a good one?"

Jessica smiled in memory. "I think so. I know my judgment hasn't been that great lately, but I sensed something special about him."

Katherine hoped he was as special as Jessica described. Her friend was due for a change of luck in the romance department. "Does he have a name?"

"Subtle, Katie, real subtle. Do you plan to put out an all-points bulletin on him?"

"Depends." Katherine grinned. "What's his name?"

"Well, not that it will do you any good..." She paused, her eyes softening. "John Lewis."

"What's he like?" Katherine prompted.

"Who?" Elliott asked as he flopped down on the quilt.

"John Lewis," Katherine replied, noticing that Elliott went suddenly still.

"Oh, she's just being the eternal optimist-matchmaker," Jessica replied. "I met him at the coffee shop this morning and I'll probably never see him again. But you know your wife. Never say die when there's one unattached male left on the planet she can possibly fix me up with.''

Elliott looked at Jessica. "I thought you were dating Rod."

"True. But since that doesn't seem to be shaping into one of the great romances of the century, Katherine is still on the trail for available fix-up material."

"She's a determined hunter," Elliott agreed, his careful gaze shifting between the two women.

"Let me guess." Katherine laughed. "That's how I caught you."

He shrugged with mock humility. "You said it, not me."

Katherine joined in the laughter, but she noticed that Elliott still seemed tense, almost as though he was on alert. She wondered why.

Jessica stretched and stood. "I think I'll check and see if our astronauts need any help reentering the atmosphere."

Katherine held up a plastic bag filled with Oreos. "Better not forget their fuel."

Laughing, Jessica accepted the bag. "Enough sugar and they *will* be in orbit."

Her forehead furrowing in concern, Katherine watched as her friend walked away.

"Problem?" Elliott asked, stretching out his legs.

"Not really. I just hate to think that Jessica's dating Rod simply so she won't be alone."

"You can't fix everything, funny face."

"No, but I can't stop wanting to. I guess I kind of feel guilty," she admitted.

Elliott's gaze sharpened. "Why?"

"Because I have you and my best friend is alone." Katherine picked up his hand, absently caressing his knuckles. "I've been turning things over in my mind—" she met his eyes, allowing the love she felt for him to shine clearly "—about how I not only love you, but I respect and admire you. And that makes my love stronger and deeper." She tightened her grip on his hand. "I know this is going to sound crazy, but it's almost as if you're another person—one I love even more than before." She paused. "Certainly in a different way. A better way I think."

Elliott was quiet, then he clasped his hand over hers. "Sometimes things change in ways we don't expect or even want."

Puzzled, she looked into his eyes. "But the changes have been good. I'll admit I was attracted to your carefree side. It was a freedom I'd never experienced and I'll always be grateful you gave me that. But for the long haul I like knowing I have your strength to lean on. That's something I never had before, either, and it's a priceless gift."

"Suppose when my memory returns, I'm the old carefree guy you married. What then?"

Hearing the uncertainty in his voice, Katherine reached out to touch his face. "Then we'll deal with it. But I don't imagine this part of you will change. The accident was life-altering. I know it's difficult for you to accept—having gaps in your memory. But you can trust me when I say that the maturing is a good thing, a very good thing."

His voice was gruff. "I hope you'll always see it that way."

She smiled, content in the knowledge that all was still right with the world. Leaning forward, she gently kissed him, her lips lingering over his. "We've only begun, my love. It can only get better."

CHAPTER FIFTEEN

"YOU DIDN'T TELL ME you were investigating Jessica Appleton," Paul said as he accepted the steaming cup of coffee from John. They were meeting at the park. It was a quiet time of the day. A few older people sat on benches while mothers with preschool-age children peppered the playground area.

"You told me you wanted to pull out all the stops," John replied, taking the lid off his own coffee, then crumpling the bag he'd carried the cups in. "I took advantage of a chance meeting in the coffee shop. I don't think she suspects anything."

"Just what angle are you using?" Paul asked.

John raised an eyebrow. "Checking me out, pal?"

"No. But whatever method you used, Jessica thinks it's a different kind of interest than what you have in mind."

"Different?" John blinked. "She thought I was interested in her personally?"

"You sound pleased," Paul noted, hoping they didn't compromise his entire CIA section by their attraction to the appealing women of the East Coast.

John shrugged, but Paul caught the light of interest in his friend's eyes. "I didn't think she noticed me. Guess I didn't do my job very well."

"Or you did it too well," Paul said wryly. "And my conscience has already met its quota in hurting women." He remembered Katherine's declaration of love. The guilt still ate at him.

"I don't intend to hurt the woman," John replied stiffly. "It was a simple initial contact."

"I know it wasn't intentional." Paul felt his own conscience pricking again. "But Jessica's pretty vulnerable, and she could take your interest the wrong way."

"She could be a good source to learn more about the real Katherine," John countered. "Who better to spill your guts to than the best friend?"

Paul couldn't withhold a sigh. "I know."

"It's not like you to waffle on an investigation, Elliott."

Paul met his friend's gaze. "It's never been this personal before."

"I'm not discounting your brother's death, but it won't help him if you're killed because we dropped the ball."

Slowly Paul raised his head. "Then you *do* think I was the target."

"The status on that hasn't changed. But you remember the rules. We take preventative measures on the small, maybe even infinitesimal chance that you could have been the target."

Paul rubbed one hand down his face. "Hell, I

know that. And I know you're helping. I'm not angry at you. I'm mad as hell at myself for letting this happen."

"Even you couldn't have prevented it," John argued. "Assuming you were the target, if you had been on the plane with Matthew, the only difference is that you'd be dead, too. And as much as you don't believe it now, that would have been far worse for Katherine and her son."

"In what way?"

"If she's cleared, you'll make sure she and her son are well taken care of, because Matthew can no longer do it."

Paul tried to disregard the pain in his heart. "After she finds out the truth, I doubt she'll accept anything from me. I'll be the last person she'll want to see."

"But if Katherine isn't cleared, you'll make certain the child is cared for, and I'm sure she'd accept that."

Paul couldn't deny the dread he felt as he looked at his friend. "If I prove Katherine's guilt, I will make an orphan of Dustin. And there's no reconciling that fact."

KATHERINE WATCHED the shadows creep up the walls, the dark shapes shrinking as the rising sun gradually lightened the bedroom. As she watched, the lace curtains at the window drifted in the gentle morning breeze. The same currents carried in the scents of the magnolias, the roses and the freshly cut grass.

She couldn't sleep despite Elliott's warm body tucked spoonlike next to hers. He had abandoned sleeping in the study, now taking his place in their bed every night. But that wasn't what kept her awake.

No, that was what she'd wanted from the beginning, what she had longed for, had despaired might not happen. But she couldn't stop thinking about the bleakness she still saw in his eyes—and the extreme tenderness in his touch, a tenderness coupled with urgent desperation. She didn't understand the cause of either the urgency or the desperation. She couldn't help thinking at times he was trying to imprint his mind with everything so he wouldn't forget.

Katherine wondered if he needed to see a doctor, a different doctor. When she'd hesitantly suggested that, he'd dismissed her concerns. But something was wrong, something he wasn't telling her.

Elliott stirred, his arm tightening around her. She stroked the length of his forearm, her hand closing over his, wishing she could somehow divine the secrets he was keeping. She had learned long ago to follow her instincts. When she'd ignored them, she'd always regretted it. And now her instincts were standing on full alert. Something was wrong, terribly wrong. But how did she prod Elliott into telling her what it was?

Katherine turned to face him and reached out a hand to touch his cheek. *What is it, Elliott? What are you not telling me?* It wasn't like him to keep things from her—he'd always been an open book. But now those covers were slammed firmly shut.

He stirred again, one hand rising to capture hers, the sunlight glinting off their wedding bands. "Morning," he said, his voice husky with sleep.

"Morning, yourself," she replied, loving the way his eyes widened, then darkened with desire.

He kissed the hand he held, then raised himself on one elbow so that he looked down at her. Tenderly his fingers caressed her face, pausing at her lower lip, tracing its outline. And still his deep blue gaze held hers.

Her heartbeat accelerated as his lips moved to kiss first her brow, her eyelids and finally her lips. It was a gentle exploration. Then the kiss deepened.

The morning sun brightened further, its warmth enveloping them. Even as his touch ignited new fervor, she tasted the desperation, the hunger. What was causing his pain? His urgency beckoned from somewhere deep inside, making her want to cry out in response.

Her blood seemed to thrum as his hands stirred her passion, creating that same incredible intensity, reasoning blotted out by yearning. And her cries spilled into his when he took them over the edge. For the moment making her forget, making the worry recede. Making everything right.

"MORE GOOEY STUFF," Dustin requested from his perch on a stool, the top of his head barely reaching Paul's waist.

Paul suppressed a grin. "It's called shaving cream."

"More s'aving cream," Dustin amended.

"I guess that is a pretty tough beard you've got there," Paul said, stooping to add more shaving cream to Dustin's small face.

"Tough," Dustin repeated, carefully imitating Paul's movements with a toy razor.

Paul's smile surfaced through his own layer of shaving cream. "Kind of like you, big guy."

"Yeah," Dustin agreed in typical male fashion.

Fondly Paul gazed at the child. Despite his intentions to remain distanced, the bond between them was growing, the warmth centered in his heart increasing each time Dustin showed him more trust.

"You and Brian going to Zorak today?" Paul asked, drawing his own razor across his cheek.

"Nah. We're goin' to the park 'cause it's got swings."

Paul marveled that the child could so easily transport himself from an imaginary planet to the neighborhood park. "That sounds like fun."

"Uh-huh," Dustin agreed, squinting in concentration as he tried to match Paul's movements.

Paul swallowed a rising chuckle. "That's good, big guy."

Dustin angled his face. "Your head all okay now?"

Pausing, Paul tried to take stock as he answered cautiously. "Pretty much. How come?"

"I don't want you to go away no more," Dustin responded earnestly. His eyes, replicas of Katherine's, seemed to gaze straight into his soul.

Feeling the fissure in his heart expand into a crater, Paul reached down for Dustin, lifting him into a hug. "I know, big guy. I know."

THE COVE WAS TUCKED into a stretch of white sand beach, hidden by the rise of gently rolling dunes. Not far away a virgin stand of bald cypress and tupelo trees guarded a pathway to swamp and marshlands. Quiet and deserted, the place was obviously one that Katherine loved. She'd chosen it, after all.

No human footprints indented the sand. The few tracks on the tide-washed beach were left by hermit crabs or sandpipers, or possibly a great sea turtle that had lurched up the sand to dig her nest.

Much like the slower pace of the South Carolina life-style, Paul could almost imagine they'd carved out their own piece of paradise. But, he reminded himself, at best it was a temporary paradise.

Katherine's long tanned legs flashed in the sun as she walked confidently ahead, claiming their spot on the pristine shore. As she turned, her hair glinting in the sun, she caught his gaze and grinned. He was stunned by the force of it, the corresponding reaction in his gut.

She held up her snorkeling gear. "I can't wait to get in."

Paul nodded, not trusting the words that might spill out. Watching her, he realized that he whole-heartedly believed she was innocent, even though he hadn't gotten the results of the entire investigation yet. If he was wrong, the consequences would be disastrous.

Yet, if she were proved innocent, the consequences could be equally dire—at least for himself. He would no longer be the recipient of her dazzling smiles, her tender heart or her loving ways. He would be the last person she'd ever want to see.

"Something wrong?" Katherine asked, one hand shading her eyes from the bright midday sun.

Realizing he must have shown his feelings, Paul shook his head and dredged up a smile. "No. Just ready to hit the water."

A relieved smile eased back over her face. "Me, too."

After pulling on their flippers, they waded in. Pro-tected from the pounding surf, the cove lured many of the smaller more fragile species of sea life. The water became deeper as the underwater shelf that supported them ended. Katherine swam ahead, turn-ing suddenly to face him, the reef behind her a mag-nificent backdrop.

For a brief moment Paul was caught by a whim

of fantasy. Katherine's long hair streamed out behind her, creating the illusion of a mermaid who'd swum up from the depths of the ocean.

Responding to her siren song, Paul cut through the space still separating them. He'd almost reached her when she whirled around and swam away, fast clean strokes sending her speeding ahead. Then she turned again, her teasing grin peeking past her snorkel.

Despite her playfulness, there was an exciting sense of mystery about her. Paul increased his speed to catch up with her when she suddenly disappeared. For a moment he darted his gaze around in concern, afraid she'd come to harm.

Then she appeared again, her smile tantalizing, beckoning him to follow. He enjoyed the sleek lines of her body as she swam ahead, her beauty eclipsing that of nature's underwater display. The fish wove a pattern around her, a screen of aquatic companions.

As they continued swimming, surfacing regularly for air, Paul realized he could watch her all day. Some investigation, he told himself with disgust, knowing he wasn't furthering his cause by dallying underwater. Then he banished the thought, wanting to savor the moment, knowing the moments would soon be ending.

Katherine disappeared again and he smiled, wondering what her next trick would be. A couple of long minutes passed and his smile faded. Moving with a speed born of apprehension, Paul cut through the water. He didn't know these waters, but he guessed something had trapped her. Twisting his head from side to side, he scanned the area, not seeing a trace of her. His heart was settling into a painful rhythm. He refused to let himself believe it was the same signal he'd felt about Matthew.

Resisting the urge to panic, Paul swam a wider circle. His training kicked in, every instinct on alert as he searched in a methodical pattern. But his rapid pulse and straining lungs warned him that he was running out of time to find her.

Then he spotted it.

A glimpse of red, Katherine's bathing suit, one he had studied at length as they'd walked to the cove. Propelled by adrenaline, he was at her side in moments.

And she wasn't teasing.

The panic on her face was real as she pointed to her foot, wedged between two huge rocks.

Not wasting a second, Paul acted. Briefly he grasped her arms, his eyes sending her a message of calm, knowing it was imperative she remain composed. Then he reached for the trapped foot.

The rocks wouldn't budge. His heart slammed into his ribs as he struggled unsuccessfully to release her. Frantically he looked around and spotted a fallen branch. He swam back to it and dragged it to the rocks, then wedged the branch beneath the smaller rock, creating a lever. It took all of his strength, but the rock finally gave just enough for Katherine's foot to slip free.

Then they were swimming upward in a burst of speed. They reached the surface, gasping for air.

Once on land, Paul pulled her close and felt the trembling of her limbs as her shock receded. Her head fell limply against his shoulder.

Placing his hand over her heart, Paul felt the steadying beat, the reassurance of life, and something inside crumbled. All the barriers and safeguards he'd erected dissolved. Katherine had crept into his heart as surely as she stood in his arms. He closed his eyes in relief that she was safe. At the same time he glimpsed a fraction of the pain he would feel when he walked out of her life. Nothing had prepared him to say so many goodbyes. And goodbye was all he had left.

CHAPTER SIXTEEN

"I RAN INTO THAT GUY again," Jessica confided as she and Katherine watched their boys. At the end of the pier Elliott was patiently teaching Dustin and Brian how to fish. So far the boys liked the worms best.

Katherine pulled her gaze from them, thinking about how the bond between Elliott and her son was strengthening. It was one of the best changes in her husband. "Who?"

Jessica shot her a disbelieving look. "John Lewis. How many men do I run into?"

"Oh. Oh!" Katherine's expression brightened, her full attention now on her friend. "And?"

Jessica shrugged, the breeze ruffling her loose blond hair. "Unfortunately nothing worth mentioning. He asked me to have coffee with him."

"And?" Katherine prompted, mentally crossing her fingers.

"And we had coffee," Jessica replied dryly. "He didn't exactly sweep me off to Bora Bora."

"Too bad," Katherine said with a smile, wishing again that the right man would walk into Jessica's life.

"I know. He's really nice." Her voice softened. "We talked a lot, more than I've talked to Rod, actually. John wanted to know about my family, my friends, my interests." Jessica paused. "He has kind eyes and he really seemed interested in everything I said."

"So what's next?"

Jessica arched her brows. "That's about it, Counselor. Nothing really worth cross-examining."

"Didn't he ask if he could see you again?" Katherine tried to keep her tone light, her fingers still invisibly crossed.

Jessica frowned. "Not really. He mentioned running into each other again sometime, but I'm not counting on it."

Katherine felt her friend's disappointment. "Well, this *is* a small town. It shouldn't be that hard to manage another casual meeting."

"Next thing I know you'll have me camped out at the door of the coffee shop."

"Not a bad idea." Katherine nudged Jessica's shoulder. "Don't be so pessimistic. He wouldn't have asked you to have coffee if he wasn't interested."

"Maybe so. But he didn't seem to care about seeing me again."

"Maybe he's shy," Katherine suggested.

Jessica's brows drew together. "I don't think so. He didn't have any trouble talking. Before I knew

it, I was spilling my guts about everything in my
life.''

Katherine chuckled. "I hope you didn't tell him
about the time we tried to bleach my hair and it
turned green.''

"No, but I did find myself talking about you,
though I left out all those embarrassing episodes—"
Jessica grinned "—because I don't think he had all
day to listen.''

"Oh, fine.'' Katherine grinned, too. "I'd hate to
meet the man and know he'd learned my darkest
secrets.''

"I got the feeling he wouldn't let on if he *did*
know your innermost secrets,'' Jessica replied. "In
fact, even though we talked for a long time, it was
almost all about me.''

"Did you tell him about Rod?''

"Not specifically. I told him I'm dating someone
but that it isn't exclusive or serious.''

Katherine sighed. "Couldn't you have held back
and let that be a little touch of mystery?''

"Well, Rod has his moments. Like when he plays
with Brian, sometimes even bringing him a toy,
making him feel important.''

"I just want to be certain he makes *you* feel important.''

Jessica met her eyes. "I'm not like you, Katherine. I don't have a wonderful man I'm sure of like
Elliott. True, Rod's not my ideal, but he's someone
to go with to dinner or the movies.''

Katherine smiled. "I'm sure you know him better than I do. And you never know, maybe you'll have more than one man vying for your attention soon."

"I'm not sure I'll ever see John again." Jessica firmed her expression, not completely disguising the longing. "Just because I'm interested in him doesn't mean he returns the feeling."

"Then it would be his loss," Katherine replied loyally. "I don't know why, but I have a feeling you'll see John again." Her smile brightened. "A really strong feeling."

PAUL REEXAMINED the account books. He couldn't believe it, More money was missing. Cash. Hard to trace, nearly impossible to recover. And he'd been so sure about Katherine. Mentally he skipped through the recent memories they'd made together. She'd been loving, kind, generous—qualities that didn't add up to being a thief.

And for the life of him, he couldn't understand what she wanted with the money. She lived a fairly frugal life-style. Her clothes were good quality, but not expensive designer items. Her cache of jewelry was small. She drove a three-year-old Pathfinder. Her needs seemed simple. Then why was she funneling money from the company?

Paul wondered suddenly if there were debts she'd accumulated, ones she wouldn't want her husband to discover. He wasn't sure why he was grasping at that straw, but he needed some explanation, some reason Katherine would still be stealing.

She could be guilty. She could have fooled you from the start. The thought crept into his mind, bedeviling him.

Picking up the silver-framed pictures of Katherine and Dustin, he studied their matching sweet smiles. He felt as though he was losing his grip on what was real, what was true. Which person was she? The one who'd wrapped around his heart with her generosity and passion? Or the thief who'd masterminded a phenomenal sabotage?

For the first time he realized his CIA training would do him no good in this situation. Nothing had ever prepared him to fall in love with his subject.

"YOU'RE SURE ABOUT THIS?" John asked skeptically.

Paul hardened his resolve. "We have to use every angle we can. I've obviously lost my objectivity. I need a clear head, an unbiased analysis."

John frowned. "I thought you were certain about Katherine's innocence."

Paul pushed one hand through his hair. "I am. I was. Hell, I'm not sure. That's why I need you."

"And now you're ready to pull her friend Jessica into it, as well?" John asked with continuing skepticism.

"I realize this goes against everything I've said so far, but I have to know the truth about Katherine.'' Paul turned, staring at the kids who walked into the ice-cream store across the street. "I'd hoped we would have the results of the investigation into her former business by now.'' He shrugged. "Without them…''

"You need Jessica," John stated baldly, "and whatever she knows.''

"Exactly.''

"And you also want me to observe Katherine myself?'' John asked with a raised brow. "That could be dicey.''

"It goes to my point about objectivity. I've lost mine. I need yours.''

"So we're going to socialize together? The four of us?''

Paul couldn't dredge up even a portion of a smile. "It may be the most dangerous double date you've ever been on, my friend.''

John clapped a hand on Paul's shoulder. "And Katherine may be exactly what she seems. That would be worth proving, too.''

"Either way, this thing is going to explode in my face with nuclear potential,'' Paul replied glumly. "And I'm worried about who I'm going to take down with me.''

"The child?'' John guessed.

Paul lifted his bleak gaze, meeting John's eyes, revealing a portion of his pain. "And his mother.''

MOSS-BEARDED PALMETTO TREES poked their shaggy heads toward the darkening sky, while red and orange streaks bled into the blue-gray palette. Much like the sluggish pace of the low country, the sun sank lazily, silhouetting the fleet of docked fishing boats.

Lights strung from the piers dotted the black waters of the sea. Music poured from the street dance along with the laughter of tourists and residents alike. Food, spirits, art and entertainment. It filled the streets, mingling with the dancers. Harbourfest brought out tourists wishing for a memorable sunset, along with residents eager to reap the rewards of their respective trades.

"Anyone hungry?" Elliott asked, his arm looped over Katherine's shoulder.

"I am," she answered, enjoying the scents and sounds of the festival. "I want something from the Gullah vendor."

"Gullah?"

"It's a low-country culture—heritage, actually."

"Fine with me," Jessica said. John, who stood next to her, nodded, as well.

They moved through the crowd to the food booths. A smiling black woman took their orders, then turned to fill the plates with the delicious-smelling food.

As they waited, Katherine stroked a sweetgrass basket that was on display. "It's made by local weavers," she explained. "Also part of the Gullah culture."

"I'd like to hear more about that," Elliott commented, but his gaze was on Jessica and John.

Katherine lifted her brow in a conspiratorial gesture. "Sure."

But just then the woman had their food ready. As she handed out the aromatic portions, she spoke to them in a language that, while somewhat familiar, still clearly puzzled Elliott and John.

"It's a combination of Queen's English, American English and an African dialect," Jessica explained, smiling in return as she accepted her food.

"The Carolinas have a complicated blend of traditions," Katherine added.

"I can't quite decide if this is a Southern town or a seaside town," John admitted.

"It's both," Jessica said. "Don't the Yankees consider Boston both coastal and Eastern?"

"Touché," Katherine inserted, looking between her friend and John. She and Jessica had both been surprised and pleased when John had contacted Jessica, first setting up a date, then expressing a wish to become involved with her friends.

Seeing their attention was on each other, Katherine whispered to Elliott as they found a table, "They seem to be a great match."

He glanced up cautiously as he pulled out her chair. "Uh, yeah."

"That wasn't very enthusiastic," she complained. "Don't you like him?"

Elliott shrugged as he sat down, not looking at her. "Too soon to tell."

"Well, I think Jessica likes him. I hope he makes her forget she ever met Rod."

"Still on his case?"

"No. But I like John better."

"Your food's getting cold," Elliott said, picking up his cup of beer and downing a healthy portion.

"Oh." Katherine took a bite, wondering why Elliott was acting so jumpy. He hadn't seemed this uncomfortable since he'd first returned. Once again he looked as though he'd put on someone else's skin. "Jessica was right."

"About what?" Elliott lifted his fork.

"John does seem more interested in us than we are in him."

Elliott made a choking noise.

"Did that go down the wrong way?" Katherine asked. "Hold up your left arm."

"Why?" he asked, still choking.

"I don't know, but it works."

Obligingly he held up his arm, his gaze still on her while she pounded his back.

"Isn't that better?" she asked.

"I guess so," he admitted. "Maybe it's psychological."

Katherine sent him a teasing half smile. "I don't think so. Otherwise you'd still be choking. It must open the airways."

"Mmm."

Seeing John and Jessica headed their way, Katherine waved. As she turned, she caught Elliott's stern expression. Reaching over, she tapped his knee. "Be nice."

He gritted his teeth. "Whatever you say."

She wondered what was wrong with him. While not as open as before, still he was always cordial. But now he was scarcely disguising his annoyance. "You don't have to become best friends with him. This is for Jessica. Just put on whatever face you want him to see."

Elliott stiffened. "Is it that easy for you to do?"

Katherine didn't reply, as her attention was diverted by the other couple's arrival at the table. Soon conversation and laughter swirled around them. Caught up in the fun, she didn't notice Elliott's brooding gaze, or that more than one set of eyes watched her every action.

CHAPTER SEVENTEEN

SEAGULLS DIVED at the departing fishing boats, shrieking in the early-morning sun. Old men sat on benches. Younger men fished off the sides of the pier, hoping for the catch of the day.

John sighed audibly.

"Has it been that rough a month?" Paul asked. "I didn't think dating Jessica would be such a chore."

But John didn't even crack a smile. "To the contrary. I can see why you're in the position you are with Katherine." He paused. "But that's not why I called you."

"News?" Paul asked with a mix of hope and dread.

"Of all kinds. First, we have a new section chief, Allen Stanton."

Paul blinked in surprise. "What happened to Rogers?"

"Heart attack," John explained briefly. "Massive. He was dead before he knew what hit him."

The two men shared a moment of silence. Rogers had been a good man, a fair competent boss.

Paul cleared his throat. In their line of work they

lost many co-workers, but lately there'd been too many goodbyes, both personal and professional. "Other news? Did you learn anything from Jessica?"

"Only confirming what you know. They're loyal friends. Nothing out of the usual. When talking about you, Jessica seems convinced that your 'accident' did wonders for your relationship with Katherine. It seems they both feel you went away a boy and came back a man."

Paul absorbed this, wishing his twin could have snagged a touch of that elusive immortality. Yet, what would he have done if Matthew had lived? Walked away from the woman they both loved? But fate had taken away that choice. "Anything else?"

John frowned. "I was surprised to find that Jessica has a key to the catering-company building."

"She does?"

"It's on her key chain."

Paul considered this. "Could anyone else get hold of the key?"

"I doubt it. It's on the same holder as her house and car keys. That's why it was easy to ask about."

Paul wanted to move on to the subject that concerned him the most. "What about your own observations of Katherine?"

"I think your instincts are right on the mark." The breeze tossed his hair as John looked out at the ocean. "Unless she's an unusually accomplished actress. The fact that she's been able to convince you this long speaks for itself. And..." He hesitated.

Paul turned to meet his friend's gaze. "And?"

"We have the results of the other investigation. Her bankruptcy dealings were aboveboard. But her partner's moves were highly questionable. In fact, it looks as though she may have been the victim of her partner's greed. While she walked away with a modest sum—"

"The seed money for the catering business?" Paul interrupted.

John nodded. "Exactly. Her partner left the country with enough money to finance an exclusive resort property. Apparently he'd sold the business and collected the cash without Katherine's knowledge. It's likely he either torched the place or hired someone to do it for him. Then he collected on both his insurance policies. His primary policy was far larger than the one that matched Katherine's. Before anyone put together what he'd done, he disappeared."

"And Katherine was cleared?" Paul asked quietly.

"Yes. The mark her partner set up admitted that he didn't know Katherine was a co-owner. Her partner had claimed to be the sole owner when he sold the business."

"The cornerstone of my suspicions has been torn down," Paul murmured. "What about the banks? Anything out of the ordinary?"

John shook his head. "The safe-deposit box was

all we found. It looks as though she's exactly what she appears to be.''

Paul couldn't yet claim relief. ''Except for the money that's still disappearing from the company.''

''And you haven't proved that Katherine's the guilty party,'' John pointed out. ''There may be another explanation—the accountant, other employees…''

Paul nodded. ''True. I've thought of that often enough, but I was afraid I was letting emotion sway my logic.''

''Instead, you've gone overboard the other way? Concentrating on Katherine as the only suspect while ignoring the other possibilities?'' John suggested.

''Probably. I haven't probed too deeply into who else could be dipping into the company funds because I didn't want to be distracted from my main course of investigation.'' Paul sighed. ''If I had gone with my feelings, I would already have been checking for someone else.''

''Then it could be one of the employees?''

Paul nodded. ''In fact, there are a couple who leap to mind without any effort.''

''But you couldn't let Katherine off the hook that easily?'' John asked.

''Something like that. I was determined to stick with procedure, despite my instincts.''

''Do you still think Katherine could be behind the sabotage?'' John asked quietly.

Paul again met his friend's gaze. "I may be the world's biggest fool, but my gut's been telling me for some time that she's innocent."

"Then maybe you should listen to it. Your instincts have kept you alive this long."

Nodding, Paul turned back toward the railing and gazed out over the lapping water. "You're probably right."

"Do you want to get some breakfast?"

"No. You go ahead. I have some thinking to do."

John squeezed Paul's shoulder. "You didn't intend to fall for Katherine—don't beat yourself up about it. Matthew wouldn't. In fact, he's probably glad you're here to take care of her." With that, John walked away, the sound of his footsteps receding along the pier.

Would Matthew have blamed him? He would never know, Paul realized. Again he felt the sharp pain of his missing other half, suspecting that loss would remain with him forever.

It was time to tell her. Katherine had a right to know her husband was dead. Paul stared, unseeing, at the ocean. He could explain why he'd impersonated his twin, why it had been necessary to deceive her.

It might be more difficult to explain how he'd gone from investigator to lover. Perhaps even more difficult to explain how he'd allowed his heart to touch hers. He could only hope she would forgive his deception and accept the love he was prepared to offer.

THE PHONE RANG, interrupting Katherine. She was late getting back to the catering kitchens. A big event was scheduled for this afternoon, and she'd dashed home for just a moment to grab a fresh outfit. She considered letting the machine pick up, but the strident ringing pricked a nerve. Perhaps it was important.

Running toward the phone, she snatched it up, her voice breathless. "Hello?"

"Mrs. Elliott?"

"Yes." She didn't recognize the male voice.

"Mrs. Matthew Elliott?"

"Yes," she repeated, trying not to show her impatience.

"This is Allen Stanton, CIA."

"CIA?" For a moment she held the receiver away from her ear in disbelief. Why in the world was the CIA calling?

"Yes, Mrs. Elliott. I'm the new section chief responsible for your husband's investigation."

"Investigation?" she echoed. What investigation? The CIA? Stunned, she couldn't absorb that the CIA was actually calling her.

"Yes. Apparently my predecessor dropped the ball in relaying the results of the investigation. It appears to have been left completely open. But I feel

you should have the results. It's been confirmed that
your husband's death was caused by sabotage.''

"Death?" she echoed, gripping the receiver.

"In the plane crash. It also appears that the remains have been tagged to be held for disposition.''

"Remains?" she whispered, her knees threatening to give way. It was some dreadful mistake, some
mix-up. She'd watched Elliott leave that morning,
healthy and whole. "There must be some mistake,"
she managed to say. "My husband is alive."

There was a rustle of papers on the other end and
a lengthy silence. "No, ma'am, I can assure you
he's not." There was another considerable silence,
broken only by a further rustle of papers. "Ah, this
could explain it. Agent Paul Elliott has undertaken
the follow-up investigation." He paused again. "I
haven't read the entire file, but I can see that your
late husband's brother requested a full investigation."

"His brother?" she asked in a choked voice.

"Yes." More papers rustled, followed by yet another lengthy silence. "I haven't met Agent Elliott
yet, but I can see by the pictures that the resemblance to your late husband is uncanny." He paused
again. "They must be twins." More papers rustled.
"Yes, the birth dates correspond. I knew there had
to be an explanation."

Katherine felt her world shifting beneath her feet.
Twins? Elliott was dead and he had a twin brother?

"Mrs. Elliott," the voice sounded faint as her

grasp on the receiver slipped. "We'll send along a copy of the report. Meanwhile, please accept my condolences for your loss." He paused. "I'm sorry you had to learn about it by telephone. Apparently I was premature in contacting you without knowing all the facts. If I'd known you hadn't yet been informed, I would have arranged to see you in person." He cleared his throat, his discomfort obvious. "I'm sure we can coordinate the disposition of your husband's remains with Agent Elliott."

She didn't answer—couldn't answer. Remains? Her husband's remains?

Then who was the man she'd thought was her husband? Who had she been living with? And loving?

Pain, shock and betrayal assaulted her in equal waves. How could she not have known? How could she have accepted another man in her husband's place? It didn't matter that they were twins. She should have known.

Thinking of his story about amnesia, Katherine felt ill. He must have thought she was a fool, not questioning his story. But why had he wanted to perpetuate such a fraud?

Suddenly she remembered his avid interest in the account books, his constant preoccupation with the money end of the business. It was painfully clear why he'd instigated the impersonation. He had wanted to check her out, to see if she was somehow involved. Bitterly she wondered if he suspected her of mere theft, or if he thought her capable of murder, as well. It was apparent he believed that money had motivated her.

Further sickened, Katherine sank to the bench by the phone. She thought of her sweet fun-loving husband. Guiltily she remembered how she'd admired the changes in him, how she had loved him with a passion she hadn't shared with Matthew.

The betrayal cut with razorlike precision. Her face sank into her outstretched hands, the sobs erupting. What had she done? And why had he made her love him?

PAUL WALKED from the pier toward his car. He couldn't delay any longer. The sun had already begun its descent as he'd tried to decide how to tell Katherine. He had searched for the words, rejecting most of them. No matter what words he chose, he knew they would inflict pain.

The truth was he should have already told her. He'd delayed, knowing she would feel betrayed, knowing she would immediately ask him to leave. But it wasn't a deception he could portray forever.

His cell phone rang. Grateful for even this small delay, he slipped the phone from his pocket.

But John's urgent voice confirmed that he had no more time. The new section chief had called John about the investigation, mentioning his call to Katherine, questioning Paul's role. John had filled him in, but the damage was already done.

Katherine knew.

Closing the phone, Paul ran to his car, then sped toward the home he'd shared with Katherine and Dustin. Her Pathfinder was not in the garage. But he held on to his control as he rushed into the house.

The place echoed with silence. Still, he ran up the stairs and into the bedroom. Throwing open her closet door, he could see an empty space on the rack where her favorite things usually hung. A quick perusal of Dustin's room showed much the same thing.

Paul headed down the stairs and into the kitchen. Nothing was out of place. Its very neatness looked singularly cold. Eyes darting around the room, they landed on a stack of papers on the table, held in place by a mocking kitchen witch.

Although he dreaded to see the words, Paul picked up the paper.

Elliott, or should I call you Paul?
It's clear you thought more of money
than of either Matthew or me. I would
hate for your "investigation" to go
unrewarded. Take what you came for
and then leave.

She hadn't signed the note, but there was no doubt it was from Katherine. Slowly Paul reached for the other papers. He scanned them, his heart sinking. She had signed the catering business over to him. Giving him what she must now be convinced he wanted.

Knowing he had to reverse that impression, Paul also knew he had to find her. And there was only one person he was sure she would trust with her hideaway.

"I'M SORRY, ELLIOTT. I can't tell you." Jessica crossed to the wall of windows that looked out to the ocean.

Paul tried to rein in his frustration. "You know she's in pain, Jessica, believing the worst. I'm the only one who can explain why what I did was imperative."

Jessica's gaze was skeptical. "I think she has a pretty good idea of why."

"No, she doesn't. She thinks it's about money. But it was about my brother, discovering the truth about his death."

"Then you really do think Katherine had something to do with his death?" Jessica asked in shock.

So Katherine believed that. "I know Katherine is innocent. But I couldn't assume that before I knew her. My brother deserved nothing less than what I gave him."

"And what did Katherine deserve?"

Paul flinched. "Not what fate gave her. But I couldn't know that at the beginning."

"And now?" Jessica's gaze didn't leave his.

"When you knew she was falling in love with you? You, not your brother."

Was it wrong to feel hope at the leap of joy her words caused? He wasn't sure, but he couldn't stifle the emotion. Paul wondered if he could trust Jessica, then decided he had no choice. "Now? Now I'm in love with her."

Jessica gasped, then her eyes softened. "Truly?"

He nodded. "And I need to find her...to tell her...to explain."

"I'm not sure she'll listen." Jessica hesitated, then seemed to come to a decision. "But I think you need the chance to try and make her understand." Pivoting, she walked to her drafting table, quickly scribbling directions on some sketching paper. Then she handed it to him. "I'm not sure I understand, either."

Paul met her gaze. "That makes three of us."

CHAPTER EIGHTEEN

JESSICA'S FAMILY CABIN was tucked inland. The directions weren't complicated, but the roads twisted past marshlands, crumbling ruins of ancient shanties and groves of moss-draped live oaks. Soon the lush greenery began to take on a sameness that made Paul wonder if he was keeping on course.

But nothing would have stopped him. Despite the humidity that wrapped around the approaching twilight, Paul kept his windows open, needing all the air he could drag into his lungs. Knowing he was choking on the truth, he could only imagine what Katherine was feeling.

He rounded a bend and spotted the cabin. Katherine's Pathfinder was parked out front. Apparently she had believed that Jessica would never reveal her hiding place.

Parking his car, Paul had barely stepped out when he saw Katherine. She held a basket of wildflowers. He walked quietly toward her, seeing she hadn't yet noticed him.

Katherine's head lifted suddenly, her gaze flying directly to his, and her body stiffened in surprise. But she didn't speak.

He covered the distance between them, each inch seeming like a mile. Finally he stood in front of her. "Katherine."

Stiffly she nodded, her fingers tightening around the basket handle.

"Are those flowers to cheer you up?" he asked, not certain where to begin, knowing he couldn't simply split open his chest and show her his painful heart.

"They're for Matthew," she replied rigidly, accusation burning in her violet eyes. They reminded him suddenly of bruises, and the evidence of her crying tore at him.

"I want to explain."

"There is no excuse for what you did," she flared.

"I'm not offering excuses, just an explanation. You need to know I did this for Matthew."

She held herself rigidly. "Funny. It doesn't look that way to me."

Paul searched her face, looking for even a flicker of understanding. "How *does* it look to you, Katherine?"

"You thought I was after Matthew for his money. I saw your obsession with how much was spent, how much was coming in. You thought I had something to do with the plane crash, so I could get Matthew's money. If I hadn't been a suspect, you would have told me who you are, why you were here."

Paul looked past the anger, seeing the pain, hating

what it was doing to her. "I might have thought at first that you were a suspect, but I came to realize you were innocent."

"You have a funny way of showing it." She gazed at him, her eyes frosty. "I'm not sure why you're here. Didn't you find the papers to the catering company?"

Paul nodded, wondering what he could say, how he could fix the terrible mess he'd made. "Yes."

Katherine's voice was acid. "There's nothing left for the vultures to pick over. That's all there was. You've made a trip for nothing." She started to turn away.

He grabbed her arm, wondering how to convince her. "Katherine, wait."

She looked pointedly at his hand. "Let go of me."

Reluctantly he dropped his hand. "What can I do to convince you?"

"Nothing. You've had a world of time for explanations before today. You didn't think they were important then. I don't think they are now."

Paul shared her pain, but knew she would never believe that. "Isn't there anything I can do?"

"Leave. And forget you ever met Matthew's money-grubbing widow." Her eyes blazed. "I see how much the money means to you. That's all you were ever concerned about. That, and if I killed Matthew for it." Katherine's rage boiled, sending tears spilling onto her cheeks. "You got what you came for. I don't ever want to see you again.'' Rushing to the cabin, she slammed the door, shutting him out.

Reeling from her words, Elliott stood rooted in place as twilight thickened the night air. Why hadn't he told her sooner? And what was he going to do now?

THE CABIN DARKENED, the fire providing a soft glow aided by only one low lamp. Katherine watched as Dustin slept, his peaceful face innocent and open. His favorite stuffed toy was scrunched beside him. Bobby Bear. The healer of all ills.

All ills except the one she suffered. Seeing Elliott had been a shock equal to the CIA man's phone call.

Suddenly every difference between the brothers stood out in stark relief. The firmer chin, the bare lip, the eyes. Eyes that couldn't be the same, because the twins shared many things, but not the same soul.

How had she not seen the evidence?

As they had throughout the numbing day, her thoughts jumped from her own self-recrimination to her grief over Matthew. This time he wouldn't be coming home. How had such an enduring spirit been lost? Vaguely she remembered the mention of sabotage. But who could have wanted to hurt him? His generosity was matchless, his kindness unending.

Knowing the man she had opened her heart to believed she could kill Matthew stunned her beyond comprehension. It had taken her a while to piece together the scenario. But there could have been only one reason Paul conducted an investigation posing as Matthew. She was a suspect; otherwise, she would have known his identity from the beginning.

Paul had come in and taken what had rightfully belonged to Matthew—her trust and her love. More, Paul had made her love *him*. Despite her grief, Katherine knew her feelings for Paul were far different from those she had for Matthew. And she blamed Paul for the guilt that caused.

How could he have made her love him?

The impact of her double loss hit with unprecedented force. Matthew, who had taken her away from the painful rigidity she'd always known, introducing her to fun and laughter, something she would forever be grateful for. Paul, who had taken her to unknown heights of passion, who had become a true life partner. Both were gone. The hole in her heart expanded as the agony assaulted her.

Experiencing two such different and special loves, it pained her to know which she would have chosen. And realizing her love belonged to the survivor made it even more difficult. If she could bury the love along with Matthew, somehow it would have made sense. But that wasn't possible. For all the pain of his deception and betrayal, Katherine knew Paul's was the love she craved. Because of it, her heart continued breaking, the splintered pieces reminding her that everything was lost.

PAUL HEARD THE PHONE. Knowing it wasn't Katherine, he considered not answering. But the persistent peal continued. Thinking it could possibly be Jessica with news of Katherine, he picked up the receiver.

"I've been trying to reach you for hours," John greeted him. "Your cell phone is off."

"I was at my attorney's," Paul replied, looking at the impressive stack of documents in his briefcase.

There was a small charged silence. "Can we meet?"

Paul tried unsuccessfully to stem his impatience. "Can't we talk on the phone now?"

"Are you there alone?" John countered.

"Katherine still hasn't returned from the cabin, if that's what you're asking. I was about to head out and try to see her again. Try to convince her to come home."

"Wait for me. I don't need much time and I can be there in five minutes." John ended the call without waiting for a reply.

Paul glanced out the window. He could use another delay. Even though several days had passed, he still hadn't figured out how to convince Katherine. He wasn't sure if he possessed enough words in his vocabulary to persuade her that his intentions had been good. But would she forgive his methods based only on intentions?

Prowling around the house, Paul found himself on

the stairs, heading toward the bedroom they'd shared. Although everything about the house was empty, this was the room that mocked, even accused, him. Sterile now without Katherine's presence, the very softness of the decor seemed to demand an answer. And Paul feared his explanations would fall short.

The doorbell rang. It seemed to Paul that far less than five minutes had passed since John's call. Then again, lost in his own thoughts, he realized it could have been far more.

"What couldn't you tell me on the phone?" Paul asked, pouring them each a drink, needing something to warm the chill he felt that had nothing to do with the temperature.

John hesitated briefly. "Stanton felt bad about blabbing to Katherine. He's new, but he's also a paper pusher, not a field agent. Because of the screwup, he stepped up efforts on the investigation—put it on a full-alert priority status."

Paul's interest quickened, but along with it he felt a sense of impending dread. "And?"

John met his eyes, his own gaze somber. "A mole in the Falgetti camp confirmed that you were their target. They sabotaged the plane."

The news wasn't a complete surprise, yet it knocked the breath out of him. Paul was a key witness in the upcoming Falgetti trial. "There's no doubt?"

John shook his head.

So Matthew had died in his place. An inescapable combination of remorse and guilt swept over him. Paul knew he would never forgive himself. "I should have been…"

John interpreted the words left unspoken. "You couldn't have prevented his death. If you had been with him, you'd both be dead."

But it wasn't that easy for Paul. "And if I hadn't been working on such a high-profile case, I wouldn't have been a target."

"You've gone undercover before," John said calmly. "And you didn't have any reason to suspect this sort of assassination attempt—it goes against type for the Falgettis."

"But I'm the key witness in their case," Paul argued, feeling the double-edged pain of loss and guilt. "It was my responsibility. I should have thought of that and not endangered Matthew."

"You can't turn back time."

Paul ignored the words. "Did the informant tell you who the hit man was?"

John averted his eyes. "No. And he won't be telling us anything else."

So they'd lost that connection, as well. The Falgettis considered lives expendable. Lives such as their informant's and Matthew's. Lives the criminal family couldn't be allowed to destroy.

John glanced at him uneasily. "Elliott, I don't like the look on your face. What are you thinking?"

Paul's eyes were hard with determination. "I may

not be able to turn back time, but I can lure out a killer, put a stop to any more killing.''

The furrow in John's forehead deepened. ''Lure?''

''I'll be the bait. And we won't sacrifice the innocent again.'' Paul's unseeing gaze flicked out toward the ocean, then back at his briefcase. ''I'll contact Stanton. This time there can't be any screwups.''

KATHERINE LIFTED her head, listening. She thought she heard a car approaching the cabin. But ever since Paul had shown up, she'd imagined that sound a thousand times. She didn't want to believe it was wishful thinking. Surely she had more conscience than that.

Yet her bed now seemed incredibly lonely. Her arms had reached out a dozen times in the night, only to end up empty. The emptiness haunted her. Coupled with her guilt and sense of betrayal, she'd been able to think of little else.

A car door slammed.

For a few moments she was paralyzed. She crept toward the window and pulled aside the curtain. It was him.

Glancing at the door, she realized it was unlocked. She flew toward it.

But it was pushed open before she could reach it. And Paul filled the doorway.

"I thought you might be planning to lock it," he greeted her without a trace of apology.

How could she have ever thought he was Matthew? Her husband would never have made such an assertive move. Unable to reply, she stared at him.

"I have something for you," he said into the silence. Striding to the dining table, Paul dropped his briefcase on the wooden surface, then snapped it open.

Katherine found her voice. "I don't want anything from you."

"You don't want excuses or explanations. This is neither." Pulling out a stack of papers, he crossed the room and placed the documents in her limp hands.

She tried to scan the documents, but her frazzled mind couldn't take in their meaning. "What are these?"

"My trust fund," Paul replied briefly. "The one I shared with Matthew." He paused, watching her. "It's yours now."

Shaking her head, Katherine glanced from Paul to the papers she held. "I don't understand."

"You think I only care about the money. I tried to think of a hundred explanations to convince you otherwise. Then I realized there weren't any words you'd believe." Again he paused. "Your catering company isn't worth a fraction of my trust fund. I've signed it over to you."

She looked at him in stunned disbelief. "But why would you do that?"

"To convince you."

Again she voiced her skepticism. "Of what?"

"That my intentions were never to hurt you." One hand plowed through his hair, a gesture she now recognized as a sign of his agitation. "I admit I deceived you, but I had to know the truth. Matthew deserved no less."

His lies continued to claw at her. "This is a grand gesture—"

"It's no gesture," Paul replied. "That's an irrevocable trust." He paused, his eyes seeking hers. "I don't know how else to say I'm sorry."

Tears were choking her as her heart contracted. "This is too huge to be bridged with an apology. Your deception, your betrayal..." Katherine's words trailed off as the tears swelled.

Paul wanted to take her in his arms, to comfort her and reassure her. But she stood stiffly, like a fragile piece of porcelain, ready to crack at the slightest touch. Instead, he watched her, agonizing over the struggle he saw on her face.

"You didn't even allow me to grieve for my husband," she finally choked out between sobs.

"We both lost Matthew," Paul countered in equal pain. "And we both loved him. I've shared a bond with my twin since birth. Part of me died with him, a part I'll never retrieve or replace."

Unexpectedly she held out her hand as though to

comfort him. Startled by her own reaction, she raised her eyes to meet his, her hand lingering uncertainly in the air between them. "Why didn't you tell me sooner?"

"Guilt," he replied in a husky voice steeped with emotion. "And torn loyalties. When I first considered opening up to you, I was held back by my loyalty to Matthew."

Searching his face, Katherine looked for the truth, wondering if she could recognize it. "And then?"

Paul's jaw tightened and she watched the shifting emotions in his eyes. "Then I realized I loved you. And that stopped me. I was afraid if I told you the truth, you might never forgive me, and I couldn't bear to take that chance...to risk losing you."

Despite everything, it was what she wanted to hear. But how could she believe him? Everything they'd shared had been based on a deception. Could love rooted in a lie possibly be real? "I...think you were right. It's too late."

For the first time since he'd entered the cabin, Paul showed a trace of hesitation. "Is Dustin here?"

"He's with Brian. Jessica took them on a picnic."

"Could I see him?"

"I don't think that's wise. It's going to be difficult enough to explain two Elliotts and what happened to the one he really knew. I think you've done enough damage."

His eyes darkened. "Is that all, then?"

Pain and love tore at Katherine, shredding her

emotions into minuscule ribbons. "You know how I feel." She paused. "I don't think there's anything else to say."

"Say you'll help me."

For a moment she thought her fog of pain and shock had confused her. A plea for help, rather than forgiveness? "Help you?"

"Will you help me find Matthew's killer?"

She shook her head in confusion. "His killer?"

Paul's face hardened, matching the bleakness in his eyes. "I was the target. Matthew died in my place."

Katherine thought she'd felt all the pain she was able to withstand. Yet a new wave rolled past her defenses. "I don't understand."

"I was working on a very high-profile case. I got too close. They wanted to eliminate me, so they sabotaged the plane I was supposed to be on. Only I wasn't on that plane. Matthew was."

Katherine clapped a hand to her mouth, biting back a sob. Could there be a greater guilt than knowing his brother had been killed in his place?

As quickly, she was struck by the knowledge that his pain now concerned her more than her own. How could she think about comforting him after what he'd done? Deliberately she pulled back, reining in the unacceptable emotions. "I don't know how I can help."

"I plan to set a trap." Paul's voice remained deceptively calm. "I'll be the bait."

Despite herself, another gasp escaped. "But you could be killed!"

"It's a chance I have to take." Eyes, so grim they chilled even the warm day, met hers. "Matthew deserves no less."

KATHERINE CHOSE the location with care. It was the spot she and Matthew had taken Dustin to when the trio had gone on picnics. So many memories had been forged here. Closing her eyes, she hoped the remembrance of those good times would keep them strong in the face of this nightmare.

Withdrawing a peanut-butter-and-jelly sandwich from the hamper, Katherine offered it to Dustin.

He accepted the sandwich, immediately tasting his favorite gooey lunch. "How come Brian couldn't come to our picnic?" he asked around a sizable bite of the sandwich.

Katherine leaned forward to wipe jelly from the side of his mouth. "I told you, sticky monster. Brian's spending the day at his grandmother's."

"Oh." Content with the answer, Dustin continued chewing.

"But I did want to talk to you, sweetie."

Unperturbed, Dustin continued eating. At his age, those particular words didn't have the ominous ring they held for adults.

"You know how happy we were when Elliott came home?"

"Uh-huh."

"Well, Elliott didn't actually come home. Instead, his twin brother has been…staying…with us since the crash."

Dustin's brows drew together. "Then where's Elly-ut?"

Katherine's hands shook and she knew her voice trembled, too. "He's in heaven, sweetie."

"With Uncle Michael?" Dustin questioned.

Katherine blinked back a sudden start of tears. "Yes, with Brian's dad."

"They're together?"

"You could say that."

"That's okay then," Dustin declared in a remarkably philosophical way. "'Cause Brian says his daddy's happy all the time in heaven."

"You know Elliott's still grinning," she agreed, knowing she would always remember him that way.

"Did he send the other Elly-ut?"

Katherine struggled with the truth. "Not exactly. But someone bad may have caused Elliott's plane to crash, and that's why his brother came here."

"He's brave," Dustin announced. "He'll fix 'em."

Katherine smoothed the hair back from Dustin's forehead. "Do you have any questions, sweetie?"

"I like both Elly-uts."

"They're not exactly both Elliott—"

"Uh-huh. They're both Elly-ut. *He* said so."

"I think you'd better call him Paul."

"Okay. Is Elly-ut coming back from heaven?"

Katherine's heart contracted. "No, sweetie. He isn't. But he'll always be in our hearts."

"Is Paul going to heaven?"

Another wave hit her. A bruising onslaught of pain. "Not yet, sweetie."

"I like the new Elly-ut."

"Paul," she corrected, feeling immediately guilty for silently agreeing with her child.

"And you're sure he's not going to heaven?" Dustin persisted.

"Not if he stays safe," she assured him warily, since she knew about Paul's dangerous occupation.

"Are we helping him stay safe?"

The pain refused to relent. "Would you like that?"

Dustin's head bobbed earnestly in assent.

"Okay, then. I guess we'd better help."

Dustin relinquished the remainder of his sandwich to fling sticky hands around her in a hug. "Promise?"

She hesitated.

"Promise?" Dustin insisted.

"All right." Desperately Katherine returned his hug, vowing to keep her son safe. And hoping she could keep her promise.

CHAPTER NINETEEN

THE EDITORS of the local newspaper preened as their story was picked up by national wire services. While Combined Catering had a share of local notoriety, it wasn't anything compared to the interest after the splash in the newspapers.

The article announced Matthew's death and the fact that in cooperation with the local police his twin brother had "taken his place." The article went on to say that the deception had been engineered for the purpose of discovering whether there had been any sabotage connected with the crash. It concluded that the crash had, in fact, been nothing more than an unfortunate accident, and that Paul would remain in their small town to continue operating the catering company. The newspaper had readily accepted Paul's version of the facts, not realizing they were announcing his trap to the Falgetti family. And with the CIA's assistance, the article went global.

Although the employees at Combined Catering were initially stunned, they seemed to believe Paul's explanation—that he and Katherine had been working together with the authorities to learn what had happened to Matthew's plane in the event that it had involved foul play. They glossed over the fact that Paul still remained in Katherine's life, making it seem like familial duty. He'd become a crucial player in the business so it was believable. But to not arouse further suspicion, it was critical that Paul and Katherine appeared to be on good terms.

No mention was made of Paul's status as a CIA agent. That wasn't something they wanted to become public knowledge. The agency was confident that the Falgettis would quickly hear Paul was alive, and so had installed a small army of agents for protection. Although returning Paul to his home base was discussed, the director felt the trap was more effective set on the deceptively innocent Carolina shore. He thought the Falgettis would assume Paul was more vulnerable in a family situation, his attention diverted by concern for Katherine and Dustin. Also, the Falgettis would be pushed to learn for certain which brother had been killed in the crash.

To Katherine's consternation, she soon learned that everything in her life was under scrutiny. Every moment, every action was watched, considered and analyzed. Although Paul was accustomed to the pressure, Katherine found it unnerving. To make the planted story appear believable, she and Paul had to behave amicably. That meant performing day and night for employees, clients and acquaintances, since they believed Paul and Katherine had been working together all along. If they acted like antagonists, the cover would be blown.

Katherine had agreed to be part of the ruse with great reluctance. She shared Paul's wish to bring in the killer and avenge Matthew's death. But faced with the reality, she wasn't certain she actually wanted to lure a murderer to their home or business. What if one of them was hurt, even killed?

She wanted to believe her only concern was for Dustin, but Katherine knew she was equally worried about Paul. If the murderer found him, Paul could be killed.

He had assured her they were in no danger. He told her confidently, without resorting to bravado, that he had been trained for this and more. Additionally agents discreetly covered the house, prepared with an arsenal of defense.

But no one was protecting her heart.

Prepared to despise the man who had deceived her, instead, Katherine found herself longing for what they'd shared. Railing at herself, she blasted each emotion, wondering how she had come to this amoral state—a woman wanting the man who had tricked her and stolen the life she'd known.

Yet each night when Paul entered the study to sleep alone, Katherine's empty bed mocked her. Yearning, sharp and sweet, filled her, making her want to shed her shell of anger. But anger was the only thing she had left. Without it she suspected she would crumble. She could just picture herself choking on the dust of her capitulation.

So her bed remained empty. Tauntingly, mockingly empty.

What had she done to deserve this fate? To have loved twice, only to have both snatched away? She knew she could never forget the mammoth deception Paul had perpetrated. How could she forget his actions? How could she reconcile her traitorous heart?

Nearing Jessica's house, Katherine followed the path that had always provided solace before. Deciding the back door was friendlier, she altered her steps. The French doors were propped open, allowing the afternoon breeze to enter.

Accustomed to entering unannounced, she didn't pause. But once inside, she halted. Crying. It was coming from the corner of the room. Her eyes adjusted to the interior light and she spotted Jessica, curled up in a wing chair.

"Jess, what is it?" She rushed to her friend's side. "Is it Brian?"

Jessica shook her head. "Just stupid me," she managed in a choked voice.

Katherine stroked the hair back from her face. "Why would you say that?"

Jessica took a deep breath, her voice quivering. "Because I thought John really liked me."

It took Katherine a moment, but then it registered. Caught up in her own pain, she hadn't considered how Jessica would react to learning that John Lewis was also with the CIA, involved in the investigation. "I'm sorry, Jess."

"Why did it have to be him? Why couldn't he have just been a lawyer or a plumber or…" Jessica's voice trailed off, the tears taking over.

"Did he tell you everything?" Katherine asked.

Jessica nodded. "Yes, after telling me he was sure I could be trusted. He said it was only right that I should know."

Inwardly Katherine flinched, wishing John had handled this better. "As strange as this sounds, I think he was trying to be nice, to do the right thing."

"I'd rather he'd done the wrong thing!" Jessica swiped at her tears. "Then I wouldn't know that he was never interested in me, that I was probably just a big joke to him."

"I'm sure that's not true," Katherine responded, angry once again with Paul. This deception was hurting everyone.

"He was quick enough to say goodbye," Jessica replied dully. "I think that says it all."

Katherine wondered if it did. John had seemed genuinely interested in Jessica. But then, she had believed the wrong brother was her husband. Who was she to judge? She certainly didn't want to voice any false hope. Jessica had suffered enough without adding that to her pain. "Oh, Jess."

"I was right all along," Jessica sniffed. "I should have stuck with Rod."

Helplessly Katherine stared at her.

"At least Rod didn't pretend to be interested just to get something from me. I'll be lucky if he takes me back."

Katherine hugged her friend, stifling her own response. Paul's motives may have been pure, but his deceit was causing them all pain.

AGENTS WERE CAMPED outside the house. The vehicle they occupied was switched regularly so it couldn't be easily marked as a stakeout van by seasoned criminals. So far the agents had taken the disguise of gas, electric, water, phone and cable-TV repairmen, as well as road maintenance. As a precaution they'd also wired Dustin's room. If anyone tried to get to the vulnerable child, the agents would know instantly. Their presence was both a comfort and an intrusion.

Katherine paced in front of the living-room windows, her gaze repeatedly drawn to the van. Today they had the telephone-company logo on it. She realized that all the prank calls she'd received after the crash had no doubt been from the agency, hanging up when they reached her, rather than Paul.

She doubted it really mattered what disguise they used. Would a professional hit man be deterred? she wondered. Or would he sweep past the agents as though they were annoying insects? Katherine wasn't certain if her fear was fueling her tension or vice versa. She only knew that her nerves were tightly strung, ready to give way at the slightest provocation.

"Still watching the watchers?" Paul asked quietly from the doorway.

She didn't turn around. "I think I'd go crazy stuck in a van for hours on end."

"It's not the best part of the job," Paul acknowledged.

"Eavesdropping, spying... It makes me cringe."

"Think where we'd be if no one was willing to do the job," Paul countered. "Would you prefer a society ruled by thugs?"

"No," she replied shortly, her anger and frustration disproportionate to the situation, yet very real. "But I would prefer not having my every movement scrutinized. I'm not the criminal."

"It's necessary," he replied quietly. "And they're watching you as a possible victim, not a criminal."

"This may be normal to you, but I'm not accustomed to being watched—to having everything I do considered, analyzed and digested," she retorted, barely hanging on to her control. She didn't know how much longer she could tolerate this. Having Paul in the house—close enough that she remembered his deceit and, because of it, too far away to touch.

"I told you this would be the rough part," Paul answered. "The waiting is never easy."

She met his gaze, her own tortured feelings relentlessly assaulting her. "But this isn't the rough part."

Her meaning vibrated between them.

He took a step forward. "Katherine..."

Shaking her head, she retreated. "I don't know how long I can keep this up. I've had enough of pretense."

Paul flinched at the remark, but she found no satisfaction in the jab. She could see the pain in his face, the remorse, even the guilt. But her own regret, guilt and sense of betrayal couldn't let her forget— or allow her to let him forget.

"Katherine, it really isn't wise to stand in front of the window," he answered, his voice devoid of the emotion that had passed over his face. "You're making yourself an easy target."

She whirled around angrily. "I thought you said your CIA buddies would protect us."

He closed the distance between them in a few rapid strides. "I didn't say they could make you invincible. You have to use your common sense."

Katherine's throat closed and she felt the sting of unshed tears. "I'm not sure I have any left." She paused, her lips trembling. "In fact, I'm not sure I ever had any."

Paul reached for her, his hand brushing the soft curls by her cheek. "Oh, Katherine."

For a moment she closed her eyes to the truth, accepting the strength in his touch. But reality quickly returned. Shaking off his hand, she stepped back, needing to hurt him in equal measure. "I don't intend to put on a display for your friends."

Visibly wounded by her words, Paul also withdrew. "Don't take unnecessary chances. You won't help yourself or Dustin by becoming a target."

Katherine watched him leave, her emotions fraying further. Knowing he was right, knowing that was never the issue, she retreated from the window. Despite his deception, she still felt guilty for the unwarranted taunts she'd just made. He hadn't intended on a display. She knew that. But she wanted to strike back, to wound him as much as she had been wounded.

Suddenly she had a vision of Matthew's irrepressible grin. And just as suddenly, she knew that Paul's pain was equally deep. Now that she knew they were twins, she could see that each possessed the other's missing qualities. To have shared that bond and then lost it must cause great emptiness. An emptiness relieved only by guilt, she surmised. The guilt of knowing Matthew had died in his place.

Yet she couldn't forgive him. Although logically Katherine understood why Paul had undertaken the deception, she still didn't understand why he hadn't told her the truth earlier. She could easily think of numerous opportunities he'd had. Yet he hadn't taken a single one. Paul said he'd waited because of his feelings for her. But shouldn't those feelings have demanded the truth?

She couldn't prevent herself from glancing out the

window one more time. How long would it take to spring this trap? Regardless, their days were numbered. And once she said goodbye, would she really know the man to whom she bade farewell? Or was that an act, too?

PAUL PULLED into the driveway of Combined Catering, then drove around to the back, wanting to use the more private entrance. He didn't need to look in his rearview mirror to know he was being followed. Accustomed to the procedure, he was neither reassured nor annoyed by the constant shadow. It was necessary, and most of the time, the practice worked. He had enough faith in his fellow agents to believe they would protect Katherine and Dustin. That was his foremost concern. But he also knew there were chinks in even the most formidable armor. For that reason, Paul intended to make sure the Falgettis had plenty of access to him when he was alone.

Normally he wouldn't have returned to the office after an event, preferring to wait until the following day to bring in the cash receipts. But this was an ideal opportunity to be a lone target for the Falgettis.

The other employees had brought back the dishes, supplies and remaining food. The darkened kitchens were orderly and clean. The staff was good, he knew, and loyal to Katherine. It was something he should have acknowledged earlier; perhaps then, he wouldn't have backed himself into such an impossible corner. Apparently his life was to be based on nothing but remorse.

A quick survey told him the building was empty, which should have been an easy assumption. But with the Falgettis' chilling history, nothing could be assumed.

Easing into the creaky chair in his makeshift office, Paul couldn't withhold a sigh. What if he had taken an entirely different approach to his brother's disappearance? Suppose he had gone to Katherine with what he knew and enlisted her aid. Would they be closer to nailing Matthew's killers? And would there have been a different resolution? Or would he still be walking away from her?

Realizing he would never know, Paul reached for the drawer handle. As he glanced down, he paused. A bit of paper stuck up slightly at the edge of the drawer. Frowning, he knew nothing had been out of place before. Instincts engaged, he cautiously eased the drawer open, watching for a trip wire. But the drawer slipped open without a hitch. Still, Paul was suspicious.

The paper that had protruded belonged in the file folder behind the one containing the cash envelope. His brows drew together as he examined the remainder of the drawer. Everything else was in place.

Then he pulled out the cash envelope. Although most clients paid by check and some by credit card or account, some occasionally paid the bill in cash. And often functions opted for a cash bar, allowing guests who wished to drink to pay for the privilege. So at times there was very little in the envelope. At other times it contained a considerable sum. Paul hadn't changed the practice of one weekly deposit. It had seemed sufficient.

Picking up the cash envelope, Paul realized he hadn't been wise in continuing the practice. This week, the cash intake included a complete wedding reception. And the last time he had handled the envelope, it had had a significant heft from the large amount of cash. A heft that was now missing.

Usually he and Katherine were the only ones to handle the cash. Several times when he had prepared the deposit, there had been more cash in the envelope than he'd anticipated. He hadn't thought about it, knowing Katherine added receipts to the envelope, as well.

Painfully Paul remembered hanging on to his suspicions about Katherine based on the missing money. But he had come around to John's way of thinking, believing that if she was taking money, it would be in the form of checks, not cash. He also remembered John had suggested that perhaps someone in their employ was the thief. *So much for loyalty,* he thought, as a burning anger started growing.

His sense of justice extended beyond Matthew to Katherine. If one of the employees had been stealing cash from the business, leaving a trail that pointed to her, he intended to find the thief. But this time he wasn't going to exclude Katherine from his investigation. She knew these people best. No one else was more qualified to say which one couldn't be trusted.

"NONE OF THEM," Katherine repeated, clearly appalled. "I trust the people who work for me. No one's given me a reason not to."

He admired her loyalty, even though her naiveté was frustrating. "I know you like everyone. But that's not pertinent—"

"Since when?" she interrupted. "It seems to me their character is the issue."

"Not everyone is what they appear," he said.

"I'm painfully aware of that," she responded dryly.

Paul flushed at the implied insult. "Not as aware as you should be. You're right about one thing— I'm not what I appeared to be. Think long and hard before you determine the same for your employees."

Her gaze met and held his. "So you want me to look at them as I looked at you?"

The implication was obvious, but now wasn't the time to tackle that one. "See past the surface," he replied, wondering if she ever had with him. If not, then perhaps to her he was only a pale copy of his fun-loving brother.

"The surface?" she echoed.

"Do any of them have a pressing need for money? Anyone with a gambling problem or a family crisis or an unexpected debt? Has anyone seemed preoccupied or acted uncharacteristically?''

Katherine frowned. ''Not really. I suppose most people could use a little more cash, but no one has come to me for a loan lately.''

''Has anyone done that in the past?''

She nodded. ''Sure. Chefs aren't generally known for their business acumen. But they always paid us back. A few times it took a little longer than expected, but nothing unreasonable. Just an extra pay period or so later.''

Puzzled, Paul stared at her. ''I didn't see any paperwork or anything on the books to reflect employee loans.''

She shrugged. ''It didn't seem necessary. Our business is like family. You don't steal from family.''

How like her, Paul realized, to float loans without even a scrap of paper. Yet her trust hadn't been foolish—until now. He hated to remind her of that, but it was necessary. ''Someone has.''

Obviously dismayed, she dropped her head, her chin nearly touching her chest. ''Maybe you're confused about the cash envelope. I can't remember from one time to the next how much money's in it.''

Paul hadn't wanted to reveal the crux of his suspicions, but she was leaving him no choice. ''There's been a steady drain from the company, Katherine. I can't be certain when it began, but it's been continuing since I started examining the books.''

Katherine's head whipped up. Her eyes met his and he could see she'd grasped the implication. ''So that's why you thought I had such an interest in money. You thought I was the one stealing it!''

''I didn't know who was stealing,'' Paul admitted. ''But I did know the thefts were taking place.''

''And why not suspect me?'' she concluded accurately. ''After all, what's a little theft to a woman who'd plot to murder her husband for money?''

''I didn't say that,'' Paul responded, knowing it was a futile defense.

''You didn't have to,'' she said tightly.

Staring into her eyes, Paul didn't see the anger he expected. Instead, her beautiful violet eyes were filled with sadness. Overwhelming incredible sadness.

''Katherine, I didn't know you then.''

''And now?'' she asked quietly, her voice devoid of hope.

''Now I know what a fool I've been, but I don't suppose that changes anything.''

She shook her head sadly. ''There was a point when you could have reversed what you'd begun, but you still weren't sure. You looked at the figures in the books, instead of what was in your heart. Love isn't black and white. It's not even gray. It's a burst of colors that can't be contained in neat categories. And you were still trying to categorize. It never occurred to you that I might not fit into one of your compartments.'' Once again her eyes, as she lifted them to meet his, resembled great bruises. ''Apparently it never occurred to you, either, that Matthew might have chosen well. Did you have so little faith in him, too?''

Paul felt the double punch of her words. Was she right? He'd assumed Matthew had again made a poor choice. Now, knowing Katherine, Paul realized how very well his brother had chosen. Matthew could have searched the world over and never found a woman more warm, giving and passionate.

With a sinking sensation, Paul knew this realization was hopelessly late. And all the regret in the world wouldn't change that. It only pushed them closer to goodbye.

CHAPTER TWENTY

THE NIGHT WAS WARM, interrupted by ocean breezes that tantalized with promises of cool relief. The employees of Lincoln Savings and Loan didn't seem to mind the heat as they filled the patio of the reception area for their annual company party.

Katherine was grateful for the relaxed pace of the function. With all the strain, it was difficult enough to manage the easy jobs. She glanced around and her gaze rested on Rod Dennison, who was tending bar. The client had requested a cash bar, which was fairly typical of most company parties.

It had occurred to her, after Paul had revealed the missing cash, that Rod could be a suspect, since he was their newest employee. Katherine had never completely shaken her initial impression of him, although she'd never discovered anything concrete to support the feeling. And a very vulnerable Jessica still needed his attention, now more than before.

Katherine frowned, thinking of what she hadn't told Paul. Alice, one of the cooks, had an ailing mother who was draining most of her finances. Alice had been forced to hire day help to watch her mother, and Katherine knew that had strained her budget to breaking point. She found it difficult to suspect Alice, but she also knew that in desperate situations, people often acted uncharacteristically. But she wasn't ready to confide that to Paul. Alice couldn't take the additional pressure of an investigation right now.

Stubbornly Katherine set her chin. If Paul could keep his secrets for months on end, she could keep a few of her own. Such as how Carter was always broke, despite two significant raises. Again her gaze rested on Rod. Was he just too smooth? Or something worse?

"Think it's him?" Paul asked, appearing beside her, holding a tray of fresh fruit that he added to the buffet.

Trying not to let his presence rattle her, she shrugged casually. "He does have access to cash."

"He's on my list, too," Paul admitted. "But the night I discovered the missing cash, he'd given me a stuffed bag of money from the evening's bar proceeds. Instead of taking the risk of stealing from the office, why didn't he just lift some of the bar money?"

"To throw you off the scent?" Katherine suggested.

"Maybe. But there also weren't any signs of a break-in at the building. Whoever took the money had to do it during business hours when the doors were unlocked. For the most part that eliminates Rod."

Katherine sighed. "You're right. He rarely comes to the building—he meets us at the functions. That limits his access."

"Any other ideas?" Paul asked.

"I told you I trust my employees," she replied defensively.

"Katherine, *someone* is taking money. It's not easy to suspect people you're fond of—"

"I'm not used to suspecting *anybody*," she retorted, realizing that if she had, she might not be in so much pain now. "I suppose it's time I changed."

"I'd rather you didn't," he said, surprising her. "I think you're perfect just the way you are."

She felt her heart hitch; wishing she could trust his words. "I used to believe this was a kind world. Not anymore."

Paul's gaze probed hers. "For that I'm sorry. Perhaps you'll find a reason to believe it is again."

Katherine remained somber. "I don't think so. It's time for me to put aside all my foolish notions. Do you know that I used to believe in lucky pennies and the pot of gold at the end of the rainbow, even in four-leaf clovers? Well, no more."

"I'd hate to think I took all that away from you," Paul replied, his voice husky with unspoken emotion.

Katherine wondered if there should be a cutoff for regret. Meeting Paul's eyes, she saw the pain, glimpsed the remorse. And knew that for the moment it was time for compassion. "Didn't you tell me that we're supposed to be behaving normally?"

Distracted, he blinked. "Yes."

"Then we should end this serious discussion. It doesn't blend with the party."

"And that's important," Paul agreed, taking her lead. "To be really convincing, I think we should have at least one dance."

Katherine couldn't reply. Instantly she thought of her yearning to be in his arms again. To whirl around the dance floor and then part again as strangers seemed impossibly cruel. "I don't know."

Paul held out his hand. "For appearances?"

For many reasons, not one of them being appearances, she accepted his outstretched hand. The music was silky and slow. It defined the texture of the night, much like the rich scent of slow-blooming magnolias, and the moon that dipped precariously low as though it, too, was tempted by the earthbound.

Then she was in his arms. Paul's touch was at once both familiar and newly exciting. Closing her eyes to the emotions assaulting her, Katherine followed his lead, their bodies fitting easily, moving easily.

She tried to stifle the yearning, biting down on a cry of rightness. It would be easy to voice the words that would make everything all right, to accept the unacceptable. But she was silent—unable to forgive, unable to step away.

Her blood stirred. Unlike the languid night, it ran hot and unchecked. Despite the arguments of her mind, her body responded to his. She should be repulsed, Katherine thought desperately, inching even closer to him. For all that was wrong, it seemed amazingly right to be in his arms. How could that be? How could his touch inflame like no other?

She felt the warmth of his breath on her neck, creating a shiver that ran the length of her body, then settled deep inside, doing dangerous things to her pulse.

The music ended. For a long moment they didn't move. Couples passed by, leaving the dance floor. Finally Katherine and Paul pulled apart and walked inside.

Feeling bereft, Katherine allowed Paul to guide her, his hand at the small of her back. They passed through the doorway to the main ballroom and Katherine struggled to make a nonchalant remark, but nothing emerged. Thinking of escape, she turned toward Paul—but suddenly his arms were around her, yanking her off her feet.

They hit the floor, hard, at the same time as a resounding crash. Dazed and stunned, Katherine stared first at Paul, then just a few feet away to the shattered remains of the ballroom chandelier.

''Any closer and we'd have been killed!'' she gasped, automatically running her hands over Paul, checking to see if he was hurt.

Paul's hands loosened their grasp. "I didn't mean to be so rough."

Shakily she clung to him, shock insulating the pain of any bumps and bruises. "Rough? You saved our lives."

People swarmed around them. Katherine thought she recognized some of the agents who were protecting them.

The horror struck then.

This wasn't an accident. It had been a deliberate attempt on Paul's life. The fact that she would have been killed, too, hadn't swayed the assassins. She raised her terror-filled gaze to Paul's and saw the grimness that confirmed her suspicions. As long as she participated in this trap, she was in extreme danger. Heart and body—both were taking great risks.

JESSICA FLUTTERED ANXIOUSLY around the kitchen, preparing tea. Because she was caring for Dustin, she'd quickly learned about the incident.

Paul had brooked no arguments about driving Katherine to Jessica's so they could pick up Dustin. Katherine hadn't put up much resistance.

Jessica glanced out the window as she brought the tray into the sitting room. She had insisted on serving tea, wanting to calm them down before they woke Dustin. "That car on the street—agents?"

Paul nodded. "They're with us."

Jessica smiled weakly. "I thought so."

"Did you have any unexplained calls or visitors tonight?" Paul asked casually.

But Jessica wasn't easily fooled. She paled, the hand holding the teapot trembling. "Do you think someone would come here?"

"I'm the target," Paul told her, "but my training says take no chances, leave nothing unturned. I'm going to request that an agent be stationed here round the clock, but only as a precaution."

Jessica's worry eased a bit. "Knowing the boys are protected will be a relief."

"It's really only a precaution," Paul emphasized. "They have no reason to harm the children."

"I know, but it still makes me feel better. And I'm glad you're here to take care of Katherine." Jessica's glance rested on her friend. "I don't want anything happening to her."

"Don't fuss, Jess," Katherine protested. "We weren't hurt, just shaken up." She glanced pointedly at Paul. "Some of us are like cats, and have more than one life."

Jessica caught Paul's gaze and sent him a sympathetic glance, before turning to Katherine. "Sounds like it was too close a call, Katie."

Paul watched their interaction, thinking again that he could have learned a great deal about Katherine from this friendship. But he'd been too cynical to accept anything at face value.

A short time later they were able to leave. With Jessica still fussing over Katherine, Paul picked up

Dustin and carried him outside. Warm and baby soft, Dustin snuggled close in his arms, his face trustingly against Paul's chest. At the car Paul hesitated. He stroked the silky hair away from Dustin's forehead, feeling both protective and possessive. Even though Paul had tried to distance himself, he'd grown too close to the little boy. Reluctantly he eased Dustin into the child seat, knowing how difficult it would be to leave him, too. He was getting damned tired of saying goodbye.

A SOLICITOUS JESSICA lingered on the doorstep after they said good-night. Heading toward the car, Katherine paused and watched Paul with Dustin. She saw the gentleness in his touch and realized that he had grown genuinely attached to her son. His reluctance to relinquish Dustin was equally telling.

Cautioning herself not to make too much of it, Katherine hurried down the path to the car. She reached for the door handle, but Paul beat her to it. Their eyes met as Katherine stepped behind the opened door. Longing and something else lurked in his expression. Unwilling to think about those feelings, Katherine dragged her gaze away and hastily climbed into the car.

In moments Paul skirted the hood, put Dustin in the child seat and joined her. But Katherine didn't want to meet his eyes again, so she deliberately kept her gaze averted.

Paul started the car and eased it onto the street.

She noticed that he looked in the rearview mirror periodically, no doubt checking for the agency car. She resisted the shudder gripping her.

Glancing over at her, Paul spoke quietly. "Are you okay?"

She nodded. "Sure."

"In the morning I'll relocate," he told her. "It's too dangerous for you and Dustin."

"What?"

"I'm not going to put you and Dustin in danger any longer. I'm the bait. There's no need for you—"

"We're in this together," she protested. "You can't back out now. I plan to do my part to catch Matthew's killer."

"That's what I want, too, but not enough to risk you and Dustin," Paul replied.

Katherine felt her heart hitch, both at the danger he was in and the protectiveness he'd voiced. She was certain of one thing—Paul shouldn't do this on his own. She knew he'd take more chances alone than with them. "The trap's been set. You can't change it now."

"I can and I will," he said firmly.

"And suppose you do?" she asked, certain he intended to take chances that might get him killed. "And suppose the Falgettis come after Dustin and me and you're not there to protect us?"

Paul whipped his head toward her, searching her expression, before glancing back at the road. "The

Falgettis have no reason to harm you or Dustin. You don't know anything that could jeopardize them.''

''They don't know that,'' she said, guessing that would push his buttons.

The silence thrummed between them for several moments.

''I don't understand,'' he said finally. ''Why do you want to do this? Matthew wouldn't have expected it of you. He wouldn't have wanted you and Dustin in danger any more than I do.''

''Maybe you two were more alike than you ever realized,'' she observed.

His voice was hoarse with emotion as he said, ''Maybe we were. I just wish I hadn't waited until it was too late to discover that.''

CHAPTER TWENTY-ONE

"YOU'RE CERTAIN?" Paul said.

"There's no doubt," John replied. "The chandelier was tampered with. By the time we found the entrance to the catwalk over the ballroom, the perp was long gone."

"It seems out of character for the Falgettis," Paul mused. "They usually use a more direct method—like a gun."

"Not always," John reminded him. "Don't forget—they sabotaged the plane. That was a first."

Paul's eyes were grim. "Great. So, they're branching out. I'd hoped the plane was an exception."

"My guess is they want the hit to look like an accident, making it harder to trace back to them. You're a key witness, Elliott. They won't want to make it obvious they're the ones who knocked you off—it wouldn't look good to a judge."

"That's reassuring," Paul said dryly.

"It wasn't meant to be. But it does mean your bait attracted the Falgettis."

Paul crossed to the picture window, ignoring his own advice that the position made him an easy target. "I want Matthew's killers, but I don't want Katherine or Dustin to get hurt."

"We're close," John warned. "I understand your concern, but this isn't the time to waffle. Surely Katherine understands that."

"Too well," Paul admitted. "I tried to convince her that I should relocate, removing the danger to her and Dustin, but she wouldn't hear of it."

"Good for her. She's made of strong stuff." John hesitated, then asked, "Do you know how Jessica's handling things?"

John's casualness didn't fool Paul. "She was shaken up when she heard about the chandelier incident, but I told her we'd put an agent on her house as a precaution."

Concern furrowed John's forehead. "Has something else happened?"

"No." Paul studied his friend's face, realizing John's interest was more than superficial. When had that happened? Paul knew John had been attracted to Jessica; he hadn't known his friend's emotions had become involved, as well. "As I said, it's only a precaution since she takes care of Dustin."

"Who's the agent assigned to her house?"

"Forrester. He's a good man."

John nodded reluctantly. "I can swing by periodically, as well."

Paul met his eyes. "One of us has to keep a cool head, my friend."

"Of course," John replied stiffly. "I was only thinking of Jessica's welfare."

"Which isn't in jeopardy," Paul reminded him. "I'm the target and I seldom visit her home. Katherine picks up Dustin. I insisted on going with her after the chandelier incident because I thought Katherine was too upset to be on her own. Don't worry, John. There was no other reason." Paul couldn't prevent the note of sympathy that crept into his voice. "And no reason for us to think she's in any danger."

John passed a hand over his face. "Jessica's a special woman. I wish it hadn't been necessary to bring her into this...to hurt her."

Paul's sigh was heartfelt. "I know exactly how you feel. Exactly."

THE EARLY-MORNING SUN warmed the sand. Joggers made their runs, implanting the first footprints of the day on the tide-washed beach.

Paul grinned at the tiny tracks Dustin left, then at the hole he was earnestly digging with a toy shovel. Paul remembered when he and Matthew had believed they could reach China if they dug deep enough. They'd believed in a lot of things back then.

"What're you hoping to reach?" Paul asked, casually glancing toward the dune, noticing the agents shadowing them, some on foot, others in a surveillance car.

"Brian says monsters live way down inside, but you gotta dig really really deep."

Paul blinked. So much for China. "And you want to reach them?"

Dustin continued digging as he considered this. "I want to see 'em."

"You aren't worried about letting them out?"

Dustin frowned. "I can't dig a hole *that* big."

"Good point," Paul said, amazed at the thinking processes of the little boy. "I guess monsters need a pretty big opening to get out."

"Uh-huh." Dustin continued his quest.

"Could you use some help?" Paul offered.

"Uh-huh." He handed Paul an extra shovel. "But don't make the hole too big."

Paul nodded, then silently worked next to him for quite some time. Several discreet glances told him that Dustin was tiring. After a while, he stretched his own arms, groaning. "Whew. I'm getting kind of tired. I don't suppose we could take a break, could we?"

Dustin's face scrunched with concentration. "Okay. But then we gotta keep digging."

"Right." Paul looked at the mounds of sand created by their digging. "I don't guess you'll need all this sand to see the monsters."

"Uh-uh."

"Would you mind if I built something with the sand?" Paul asked, hoping to distract Dustin from the futile dig to the center of the earth.

''What?'' Dustin asked.

''I was thinking maybe a space station,'' Paul suggested.

''On Zorak?'' Dustin squealed.

''Yep. We could probably even build a space-ship.''

Dustin jumped as high as his small legs allowed. ''Zorak! Zorak!''

From the corner of his eye Paul noticed an agent moving closer, no doubt wondering what had caused the sudden clamor.

He had debated about bringing Dustin to the beach, but Katherine had an emergency wedding cake to prepare. The first one had been destroyed in transit. Katherine had promised the outing to Dustin, and Paul didn't want to see the child disappointed. He'd briefed the security team, who agreed it was unlikely the Falgettis would choose such an open spot. They needed reasonable cover to elude detection, and there wasn't any on the beach.

Paul filled a plastic bucket with sand, helping to form the base of the space station. Dustin followed his lead, enthusiastically patting the sand in place, then mimicking Paul's more careful movements as he formed the levels. It was inexplicably warming to Paul, having the child imitate his actions. He was also moved by the faith Dustin showed in his ability to build a space station.

It was a little thing, he supposed. But not having his own children, he'd never guessed what powerful emotions they could evoke. And he was incredibly touched that Dustin had accepted him so completely after learning he wasn't Matthew.

Though he knew it wasn't his right, not even his place, Paul wanted to ensure that this child would always be equally safe and happy. But after Matthew's killers were apprehended, he doubted Katherine would let him see the boy. She would want to put this painful episode behind her. And he would be a reminder of the worst sort.

"We hafta build the spaceship!" Dustin reminded him, his small hands patting the oval roof they'd fashioned.

"Can't forget that," Paul agreed, picking up a bucket of sand. "Wouldn't want you stuck on earth with a great space station already built."

"Yeah!" Dustin clapped sand-coated hands together.

Several minutes later Paul had a facsimile of a spaceship built out of sand, one with a seat large enough for Dustin. It wasn't perfect, but Dustin didn't seem to mind. "Think that will get you to Zorak?"

"Yeah!" Dustin said again, and patted the last of the sand in place. "But we both gotta fly in it."

"Don't you want to pilot it alone?" Paul asked with a grin, enjoying Dustin's make-believe world.

Dustin shook his head. "You gotta come. Then we'll be safe."

Paul's smile faded. "Safe?"

"Uh-huh. You won't let nothin' get us."

Ignoring the sand that rubbed off on him, Paul hugged Dustin. "As long as I can, pal, I'll keep you safe." Releasing him so that Dustin could climb aboard his ship, Paul made a silent vow to keep him safe. He only wished he didn't have to leave—that he could protect Dustin from that hurt, too.

THE KITCHENS of Combined Catering were bustling. Every counter was filled to overflowing. The Newman anniversary party was huge. The affluent couple had given them an unlimited budget to provide the finest food, imported delicacies, vintage champagne and an open bar. It wasn't the most elaborate function they had scheduled, but it was important.

Carter, who had been promoted permanently to executive chef, had worked tirelessly on the innovative menu. Now they were in the final stages of preparation. Alice, Ben and Frank scurried to carry out Carter's instructions. Several temps had been hired, some as kitchen assistants, others to supplement the serving staff.

Katherine stepped through the whirl of energetic bodies. Her own desserts had to be spectacular. But she didn't mind the work. She welcomed the distraction.

Since the night the chandelier had narrowly missed killing them, she had seen a threat around every corner, in every shadow. Katherine told herself she was being foolish, yet she couldn't stop.

While she'd never thought much about it, she'd always considered herself a person of some courage. She lived far from family, rarely depended on anyone else, stood on her own two feet. But the other night had shown her a new side of fear.

She could have accepted Paul's offer to leave. Her refusal had been a surprise to both of them. Katherine wanted Matthew's killers to be apprehended, but that hadn't prompted her protest. Knowing that Paul would deliberately put himself in more danger had swayed her. It wasn't something she wanted to examine too closely.

Katherine measured the sugar, adding it to the creamed butter. As the mixture blended, she organized the liqueurs, lining them up in the order she would need them. She picked up her marble rolling pin, anxious to roll out the dough and create layers of paper-thin pastry. There was something comforting in the familiar work, the normalcy of it, the safety. Even the roar of the huge professional mixer, along with the rattle of the beaters, was welcome.

Suddenly feeling a hand on her shoulder, Katherine screamed and whirled around, the rolling pin raised like a weapon.

Ben stepped back, looking startled and concerned. "Katherine?"

She put one hand over her chest, feeling the runaway beating. "Ben," she gasped.

"I'm sorry. I didn't mean to scare you," he apologized. ''But Carter wants to know when the truffles and shiitake mushrooms will be here.''

Guiltily Katherine remembered her promise to check on both items first thing. With everything else on her mind, she'd forgotten. She calmed her breathing. ''Tell Carter I'll check right now. If the delivery can't be here in an hour, I'll send someone to the dock.'' As she glanced up, she saw that everyone in the kitchen was staring at her. Her regular employees looked concerned and some of the temps looked frightened, others appalled. The scream must have been high in decibels, she realized in embarrassment. ''It's okay, everybody. Just a bad case of nerves about tonight.''

A few heads nodded as some of them turned back to their workstations, breaking the unnatural silence. But others still watched her. Ben asked cautiously, ''Katherine, do you want me to call Elliott?''

She smiled sadly, wishing it was that easy. ''I'm afraid that won't help.''

Suddenly she had to escape. Someone else could finish the desserts. She couldn't bear their scrutiny. These people all knew she had lost a husband and had allowed his brother to take his place. Even though Elliott had told the employees that she had been in on the plan from the beginning, she knew some of them didn't believe him. Fear and embarrassment sent her running from the building. But as she jumped into her car, Katherine knew she couldn't outrun the truth.

PAUL PULLED SLOWLY into the parking lot of the catering company, weariness settling over him. It had been a rough evening. The Newmans' party had gone smoothly enough, but it had lacked Katherine's special touch. At first he'd panicked when he learned she had run out on the staff. Their legitimate concern was unsettling.

Then Jessica had called to report Katherine's whereabouts. Paul had been prepared to go to her house, but Jessica had tactfully suggested that might not be for the best. Translation: *She doesn't want you here.* Jessica had added that Katherine wasn't up to the Newmans' party. Could he handle things?

He had, but certainly not with Katherine's expertise. All the extra unneeded equipment in the back of the car was proof enough. Paul could have returned the equipment in the morning, but he was in no hurry to face Katherine, guessing she was home by now. These days her eyes were filled with hurt and accusation.

Unlocking the back door, Paul carried the first box into the pantry. As he put the carton on the counter, he heard a faint noise. In seconds his gun was drawn, and he was inching toward the doorway, his back flattened against the wall. Peering around the doorjamb, he scanned the kitchen. It appeared to be empty, but he wasn't trained to take chances.

He crept through the darkened kitchen. Aside from the afternoon's disarray, nothing seemed out of order. Reaching the end of the kitchen area, Paul wondered if he'd imagined the sound. But the raised hair on his arms and his quickened pulse told him his instincts were correct. To his left were the storage areas; the prep room was to his right. Straight ahead at the end of the hall was the office.

He heard the sound again, more distinctly this time, and it was coming from the office. He wondered if the Falgettis were booby-trapping the building. Edging silently down the hallway, he detected movement and ducked into the rest room. Carefully he peered around the door frame and noticed light coming from the office. What he saw next made him freeze.

CHAPTER TWENTY-TWO

KATHERINE PACED the kitchen, her mug of cocoa forgotten. "There's no mistake about what you saw?"

Paul shook his head. "It was Rod Dennison. And he helped himself to a considerable wad of cash."

"He doesn't know you saw him?"

"No. The catering company is yours, so I figured this one was your call. Once I was sure the Falgettis were nowhere in sight, I decided to watch for a while. It wasn't difficult." Paul shook his head in remembered disbelief. "Rod took his time. And it wasn't because he didn't know where to look. He had the cash envelope on the desk the entire time. It was amazing—he wasn't worried at all about being caught. Instead, he was digging through other files. Hell, he was so sure of himself he had the light on."

Katherine sighed as she glanced out the window. "This couldn't have happened at a worse time."

"How so?"

"Jessica thinks she needs Rod. The thing with John knocked out the last of her confidence." Katherine laughed humorlessly. "She said she doesn't

have a man like you to count on who loves her."
In the sudden silence their gazes locked across the
room.

Katherine felt the thrum of her quickening pulse.
Love between them hadn't been mentioned since
that horrendous day she'd learned the truth. Anger
and the pain of betrayal had refused to let her believe his words.

Now the echo of his words hung in her mind,
shimmering between them.

He took a step toward her. "Katherine—"

"No. Don't say it." She felt the press of tears,
the agony of conflicting emotions. "I can't bear it."

His eyes searched hers, growing bleaker as they
registered defeat and regret.

Katherine turned away, unable to face him. With
great effort she steadied her voice. "I don't want to
tell Jessica about Rod."

"She'll know when you fire him."

"I don't intend to fire him," Katherine replied
quietly.

"What?" Paul exclaimed in disbelief. "Why
not?"

Katherine turned to face him again. "Jessica's
been hurt enough—through no fault of her own. I'm
not going to add to her pain."

The implication of her own hurt, though unspoken, was clear.

"You're going to ignore Rod's theft? Allow him
to continue unchecked?"

"Unless he bankrupts us, yes. I'm hoping he'll hang himself if we keep the cash out of his reach. But I'm not going to allow the loss of a few dollars to hurt Jessica." Her gaze hardened. "Although I'm not sure I'm doing her a favor. She doesn't need a man who lies to her."

Paul stared at her, a flash of hurt appearing, then quickly disappearing, in his eyes. "You're forgetting one thing. There were no signs of a break-in. Somehow Rod has gotten a key. That makes all the company records vulnerable."

"People versus profit?" Katherine asked. "For me there's no debate."

Paul's frustration was almost tangible. "He's been stealing from you practically since he began working for you. I'm sure his thefts account for the missing money."

"Are you angry at him for stealing?" Sadness rimmed her eyes and coated her words. "Or at yourself because you believed I was responsible?"

The silence was deafening as Katherine left the kitchen, the creak of the swinging door its only relief.

BREAKING WAVES rolled endlessly in from the sea, each one punctuating Paul's thoughts. Ignoring the discreetly shadowing agents, he walked along the beach.

He preferred the shore at night. No distractions, no pretense. The earth, sky and sea connected in a way that seemed both personal and immediate. It was a thought he had shared only with Matthew. Until meeting Katherine, he had never imagined sharing that sort of thought with anyone else. Now that, too, was ruined.

Was she right about his fury at Rod? Had he grown so angry because he had blamed Katherine for Rod's crimes? He had been so focused on black-and-white proof. What had Katherine said about the color of love? That it was neither black nor white, not even gray.

Paul had glimpsed that burst of colors she'd described, yet he'd still questioned. Doubted. Remorse over Matthew had led him to disregard his instincts and the pain he would ultimately cause Katherine. Now he carried twice the guilt.

As he walked, Paul thought, too, of Dustin, the promise he had made the little boy to not go away again. The boy would also be hurt, not understanding why Paul had to disappoint him.

Moonlight illuminated his path, teasing bits of driftwood into mystical shapes. Spotting one that resembled a winking bear, he smiled, thinking how Katherine would enjoy the image.

Loneliness struck, a stab that had him looking toward the black wall where sea and sky met. He understood how the water beckoned to the lonely, offered escape from the pain.

His gaze drifted toward the pier, the lights that relieved the utter darkness. Life and light—both held promise. He just had to find a way to make Katherine believe him.

"THAT'S BEAUTIFUL," Jessica exclaimed.

Katherine paused as she put the last touches on the wedding cake. "It is a pretty one, isn't it? After a zillion of them you'd think I'd quit getting so sentimental."

"A diehard romantic like you?" Jessica scoffed. "I don't think that'll ever happen."

Katherine picked up another of the fresh flowers she was using to decorate the cake. "And you're not? This brings to mind something about glass houses…"

Jessica laughed. "Maybe. But I can think of worse labels."

"I suppose," Katherine murmured, wondering if they were both colossal fools. Love hadn't treated either of them kindly.

"It's sure quiet in here," Jessica observed as she snitched a bite of Belgian chocolate.

Katherine picked up a cluster of frosted champagne grapes and arranged them with the flowers. "We had a wedding breakfast this morning, so everyone got here early and left early."

"Nothing planned for tonight?" Jessica asked casually.

Katherine felt a sinking in the pit of her stomach, guessing the nature of her friend's inquiry. "Nope. Thankfully we have a night off." She gave the cake a half turn. "I only have to deliver this beauty. We're not catering the reception."

"Oh, then I guess Rod won't be by," Jessica said, not completely concealing her disappointment.

Katherine's stomach sank farther. "I wouldn't think so. He doesn't come here. He usually meets us at the function."

Jessica's brows drew together, her eyes looking puzzled. "That's funny."

Katherine clipped one of the rose stems so that the blossom lay properly against the icing. "What?"

"Nothing really. Just that Rod borrowed my key to the building once so he could come in early. Must have been something special that day."

Katherine's hands stilled. She had given a key to Jessica when the building had been built, so that she would always have a spare in a safe place. That explained how Rod was able to get into the building at will—no doubt he'd made a copy. She would have to change the locks. Glancing up, she saw that Jessica was waiting for a reply. "Right, I guess so."

"I wanted to see you, as well," Jessica said. "Rod isn't my only interest."

Katherine smiled, trying to disguise her feelings. "Have you seen much of him lately?"

Jessica shook her head. "Not really. I thought maybe he'd been working a lot of extra time for you."

Debating, Katherine finally shook her head. While she didn't want to see Jessica hurt, she also didn't want to provide excuses for the man. Perhaps Rod would hang himself with his behavior. "No. Not any more than usual." She wanted to say more, a lot more, but she restrained herself. It wasn't her place to give Jessica advice on her love life. With her own track record, it was clear she was no expert on men.

Jessica glanced out the window. "Are those agents in that car, or am I getting paranoid?"

"They're agents, all right."

Jessica glanced toward the office. "Oh, is Elliott here?"

Katherine shook her head. "No, but they keep an agent at the house and the business whenever one of us is here. I guess they don't want to take any chances."

"Seems funny, doesn't it?" Jessica mused. "It's like something out of a movie. Most of the time it doesn't even seem real."

Katherine bent her head, trying to hide the stinging in her eyes.

"Oh, Katie, I'm sorry!" Jessica jumped off the stool she'd been perched on and rushed over to hug Katherine. "How could I be so insensitive?"

"It's not you," Katherine managed, swiping at the tears that had escaped. "It's just…everything."

Jessica looked at her in concern. "That says it all, doesn't it?"

Katherine sniffled and reached for a tissue. "I'm not even sure who the tears are for today. When I think about Matthew, I grieve mostly because it was such a stupid senseless loss. He deserved so much more. He deserved a long life filled with laughter. As for Paul…''

''You're grieving because you love him,'' Jessica surmised wisely. ''And you feel guilty because you do. It doesn't seem right since Matthew's dead and Paul wasn't up front with you.''

''Up front!'' Katherine snorted. ''I had to hear the truth from the CIA.''

''I know, Katie, but think of how difficult all this must be for him. He knew from day one that in all likelihood his twin brother was dead. He probably even suspected that Matthew died in his place. Yet he had to act normal for you and Dustin. At the same time he had to determine if any of the players in Matthew's life had a motive for killing him.''

''Like money,'' Katherine agreed bitterly.

Jessica's voice was gentle. ''He didn't know you then, Katie. His loyalty was with his brother. He had to learn the truth. That took time.''

''It's too bad he didn't feel he could share that truth with me,'' Katherine lamented.

''I imagine he's feeling that way, too.'' Jessica patted Katherine's hand. ''Look at it from his perspective. He's lost everything now—his brother, you and Dustin. I don't imagine that's what he wanted, either.''

Katherine felt the sadness that mingled inextricably with her bitterness. ''But that's what's happened, hasn't it?''

THE TEMP-AGENCY RECRUITER glanced at the application in her hands. "I see you have a degree in culinary arts." She raised puzzled speculative eyes. "I'm not certain why you're interested in a serving position with your qualifications."

The dark-haired man smiled winningly. "It's not always easy to turn a degree into a job."

"Without experience," the recruiter added sympathetically. "Unfortunately that's true."

"Which is why I'm here," the man explained, his thin-lipped smile still in place.

"Have you considered an internship?" the recruiter asked. "Many of the big hotels offer programs."

"Yes," he replied. "But they're not as readily available as serving positions."

She studied the application. "I hate to see anyone underutilize their qualifications."

"The truth is I need money now, not way down the road."

The recruiter nodded. "Ah, that I understand well." She smiled again. "It's the cornerstone of our business. You probably know we pay every Friday." She turned toward her keyboard. "Let me see what we have available. The Greenery Nest is looking for fine-dining servers, and the Planter has an order in for casual-dining and banquet servers."

"I understand that Combined Catering is looking for some temp servers," the man suggested.

Turning away from her computer screen, the

woman frowned. "We don't typically allow our temps to choose which client they work for."

His smile became even more winning. "Actually I have an ulterior motive."

Her brows drew together suspiciously. "Which is?"

"I'm hoping that if they see what a good worker I am, maybe they'll give me a cooking position. It's a small outfit, which could mean rapid advancement. It's the kind of place I want to see in my future."

"Of course, if they hired you on full-time, they would have to pay us a finder's fee," she mused, the line between her brows disappearing as she thought of the tidy commission on that fee.

"So we both win," the man encouraged, his pale eyes lighting with victory.

She turned back to her computer screen, rapidly typing. "You're right. Combined Catering does have an order for this weekend, and we hadn't completely filled it yet." She shared a conspiratorial smile with him. "But now we have."

CHAPTER TWENTY-THREE

THE NEWMANS' ANNIVERSARY party had been only a dry run compared to tonight's elaborate function. Rodax, a huge computer conglomerate, had booked the event to honor their star employees. The expected guest list was triple in size, the menu more complex, the setup and service more complicated.

The party had taken over the entire first floor of the Commodore Plantation. It was a huge home that had been converted to a hotel. Even though it was much larger than the Rose Plantation, it wasn't Katherine's favorite. The rooms were so strung out it made serving a nightmare, and consequently it was difficult to maintain control of the event. But in Katherine's opinion, its primary drawback was the lack of intimacy.

Unlike the Rose Plantation, which lent itself to romance, the Commodore seemed far too commercial. In a bid to compete, the plantation had sacrificed its sense of Southern grace and charm. Katherine thought it was a terrible loss.

Although they had hired several more temps, Katherine and Paul were both needed tonight. It was difficult enough to share an uneasy household. Trying to pretend they were harmonious in front of the employees took the tension to breaking point. They had no choice, however, until Matthew's killers were apprehended.

Katherine's gaze skipped over the crowd, resting momentarily on Rod. She still hadn't found a way to deal with him, but given all the stress in her life, she couldn't handle another confrontation. When the truth about him came out, she would need to be able to focus on Jessica without distraction. Since her every waking thought now centered on Paul, Katherine knew the timing was bad. Still it stuck in her craw that she was, in a sense, paying the man to steal from her.

It had been difficult to pull the evening's function together. They weren't really staffed to accommodate something this big, but the booking had been accepted before Katherine had learned who Paul really was. At that time everything had appeared golden. The increased business had seemed like a positive step in her and Elliott's future, another building block to greater success.

Katherine felt the familiar stab of pain. That had been when she'd thought Paul was Elliott, when Combined Catering had truly been a joint venture. Although Paul had signed the business back over to her, she still felt distanced from it.

Everything seemed to be shifting—values, relationships, the very substance of her life. Sometimes it was difficult even to grasp. She still woke most mornings with a sense of hope. For a few moments everything would seem normal. But that was before she remembered what had happened, before the pain hit, along with the familiar sinking in the pit of her stomach. And inevitably she would reach across the yawning emptiness in her bed, then chastise herself for the yearning.

Briefly she closed her eyes and asked herself yet again how that could be. How could she still want him?

Forcing herself back to the present, Katherine opened her eyes and walked toward the dessert table. It was early enough in the evening for that station to still be well stocked, but she wanted to be certain. The sweet tooth could be stronger than the sensible desire for nutrients. She felt a ghost of a smile. That was what had led her to being a pastry chef, her own wicked sweet tooth.

"It's good to see you smile," Paul said as he approached.

She didn't meet his eyes. "Just thinking about the strange powers of sugar."

"For whatever reason it's a welcome sight," he replied quietly.

The ache in her heart increased. How could people who had shared such grand passion now behave like polite strangers? Yet what else were they? Unable to speak over the growing lump in her throat, Katherine nodded.

Paul glanced away, as well, no doubt equally uncomfortable. "We seem to have an awful lot of temps."

"Yes," she managed. "It's more than we've ever hired before."

Paul frowned. "Do we know any of them?"

She shrugged. "Not really. They're temps. Why?"

"I'm not comfortable using so many strangers."

Katherine gazed around the crowded room. "We're surrounded by strangers. I certainly don't know all these people."

But Paul was still frowning. "The guests have a legitimate reason for being here."

"So do the temps." She wondered why he was belaboring the point.

"But don't you usually use the same temps?"

"Usually," she said. "When they're available. The agency knows the servers and kitchen helpers we've liked."

"Hmm." Paul looked at the buffet line. "Maybe I'm being too careful. But the last big event spooked me."

Instantly Katherine remembered the crashing chandelier. "You think something will happen here?"

His gaze met hers. "Not necessarily, but I can't shake the feeling that Rod was looking for something else in the office besides the cash."

"Like what?"

"Information," Paul replied soberly. "Future bookings, their locations and access."

Katherine's eyes widened. "Do you mean access to us?" She paused as realization hit. "To you? So that the Falgettis can get to you?"

"Don't put words in my mouth," Paul advised. "Rod could have been looking for information he can sell to the competition. He's an opportunist, but from what I've seen, I don't think he's smart enough to be in league with major criminals."

"Unless he stumbled into them," Katherine suggested, suddenly worried.

"Unfortunately you could be right." Again Paul scanned the area. "Point out which temps you don't know. But do it casually. If anyone isn't who they appear to be, I don't want to tip them off."

Katherine swallowed her fear. "Aren't other agents here? I mean, if someone tries something, won't they protect us?"

"Yes. But this isn't the O.K. Corral. With all the people in the building, we can't start blasting away. The reality isn't much like what you see in the movies. The bullets don't dodge the innocent, hitting only the bad guys."

Katherine's throat was dry as she bit back her fear. "Of course not." She was grateful for Paul's presence. She knew that made little sense, but wasn't about to examine why.

It didn't take them long to weave through the crowd and reach the kitchens. Although temps were part of the crew, Katherine recognized all of them. She whispered as much to Paul as they left the kitchen.

"Let's check the line," he suggested, heading back to the ballroom.

Before they could check out the other temps, Katherine heard the faint whir of the cell phone in Paul's jacket.

He grimaced. "I'd better get it."

Knowing it was his link to the agency, Katherine nodded, her gaze already scanning the few temps she could see. Nothing out of the ordinary there, but she couldn't see beyond the champagne fountain. Still trying to look casual, she turned back to Paul.

One glance at his face told her there was trouble. Serious trouble.

He snapped the cell phone shut and took her hand, pulling her toward the open French doors that led to the veranda.

Katherine faced him as soon as they were outside. "What is it?"

His eyes held a grim determination she'd never before seen. "Katherine, you have to be calm when I tell you what's going on. We're being watched. One false move could make the situation worse."

The acrid taste of fear almost robbed her of breath. "Tell me quickly." She grabbed his arms, her fingers digging in.

"They've got Dustin," he said quietly.

She swayed, feeling the blood drain from her head. "No. Oh, God, no!"

Paul reached out to steady her. "I know how difficult it is, but you have to act normal." His eyes cut sideways toward the crowded ballroom, emphasizing his meaning. He took a deep breath. "Dustin won't get hurt. They don't want him. They want me. They'll let Dustin go as soon as they have me."

Adrenaline raced through her system as she pushed away from him. "We have to get to Dustin. We have—"

"Katherine!" He pulled her back toward him. "They want me to go alone. We have to do as they say."

"You're not going without me!" she told him fiercely. "He's my baby!"

"I know that, but they'll see you leave with me. That would only put Dustin in more danger."

Katherine shook her head, thinking furiously. "They don't have to see me." When his response was a baffled look, she rushed on. "The kitchens connect to the old slave quarters. There's an underground passage beneath the pantry where we brought in the warming trays. We can split up in the ballroom. You head out to the car. I'll wait for you in the back. It's just beyond the gazebo."

"Katherine, this isn't wise. It's best for me to go alone. I'm trained to—"

"I don't care what you're trained for! I'm his mother. That outranks the CIA, the president or anything else you can think of. And if you don't take me, I'll follow you on my own!''

Paul reached out again, holding her arms. ''You would, wouldn't you?'' Their eyes met and she could read the caring in them. ''All right, it's against my better judgment. But be careful. Don't create any suspicion and don't tell anyone where you're going.''

She nodded soberly.

His fingers tightened around her arms, before he dropped his hands and turned to walk away.

''Paul?''

He looked back over his shoulder.

''How are you going to make them give up Dustin?''

His expression didn't change, except for the slight lifting of one side of his mouth. ''By giving them what they want.''

Katherine's mouth fell open as she realized his intent. Fear for her child coupled with the dread his words had caused. He intended to sacrifice himself for Dustin. And she was powerless to keep them both alive.

URGENCY PROPELLED the Porsche and its occupants through the dark night. Paul kept the speed high, expertly steering the powerful low-riding sports car around the curves. For once, Matthew's expensive car seemed worth every penny.

Katherine held her breath, but it wasn't her own safety that concerned her. "Where are we going?"

"To Jessica's," Paul replied briefly, not taking his eyes from the road.

She gasped. "Do they have Jessica and Brian, as well?"

"Yes." The solitary syllable conveyed plenty.

"What happened to the agent who was guarding the house?" Katherine demanded. "I thought he was supposed to keep them safe."

"No one's infallible," Paul reminded her. "Even CIA agents make mistakes."

Katherine recognized the implication, but didn't comment.

"I'm guessing the agent was probably overpowered." Paul hesitated, the silence between them as heavy as the humid night air. "Katherine, I misjudged the situation and made a bad call. I never expected them to grab Dustin. I should have figured they would guess he was my Achilles' heel."

She shut her eyes and leaned her head back against the seat. "I know you didn't intentionally put Dustin at risk." A sigh rumbled through her as she realized, despite everything, that Paul was a decent and good man. Not the kind of man to endanger a child. Instead, he was a man willing to trade his own life for that child.

She opened her eyes to the encroaching darkness. "And I know you'll do your best to get him back safely."

Glancing over, Katherine saw Paul's Adam's apple work before he nodded, not pulling his gaze from the road as they sped into the night.

It didn't take long to reach Jessica's house. Blanketed in the darkness of the peaceful neighborhood, it looked deceptively safe. Paul stopped the car several houses away, having already doused the headlights. It seemed incredibly quiet, as though even the crickets had suspended their nighttime chorus.

Paul dialed a number on his cell phone and quickly outlined the situation to an agent. Snapping the phone shut, he turned to Katherine. "I want you to sit tight, no matter what happens." He handed her the cell phone. "Other agents are en route, but you can always call 911."

She was shaking her head. "I'm not going to let you go in alone."

Frustration lined his face as he gritted his teeth. "This is exactly why I didn't want you to come. You're too damned stubborn."

"Which means you know I'm not going to stay here. You might as well accept that and use me to help. I'm not going to sit meekly by while someone's threatening my son's life!"

Paul sighed in resignation. "You'll have to do *exactly* as I say. This has nothing to do with your stubbornness. One wrong move could spell disaster."

Even further chilled by his words, Katherine nodded. "I know you're the expert here. What should I do?"

"I plan to talk the Falgettis into allowing Jessica and the children to come outside before I go into the house."

Katherine swallowed her fear. "Then what?"

"If they cooperate, I'll make sure Jessica and the boys are a safe distance out the door before I go in."

"Isn't there another option?" she asked desperately, not willing to allow Paul to sacrifice himself so easily. "What if we waited for the other agents to get here and help you?"

He shook his head. "The Falgettis demanded I come here alone. But lone-ranger operations are against policy. If the other agents arrive before we get Dustin out, the Falgettis will know I crossed them. That could spell disaster."

"Surely there's something else we can do!"

Paul hesitated, glancing upward at the dark sky. "If we can time things exactly right..."

"What?"

"As soon as Jessica and the boys step outside, we can cut the power to the house. I can toss in another diversion. It's so dark that a sudden blackout might throw them off long enough for us all to escape."

"I could pull the breakers!" Katherine's voice was urgent as she glanced at Jessica's home. "I know where they are—on the exterior wall near the front of the house. And I'm sure I can peek around the corner to see the door from that spot.''

He seemed to be weighing the options before responding. ''Okay, but that's all,'' he warned. ''I can't protect Dustin if I'm watching my back for you.''

She nodded and he seemed satisfied.

Paul was right, she realized, as he moved rapidly to the trunk of the car. The night was moonless, and for once she was grateful for the darkness.

In seconds Paul stripped off his dress shoes and exchanged them for running shoes. To her surprise he bent down and picked up a baseball-size rock. Then he reached into a black duffel bag, shoving several things in his pockets.

Katherine stared at the unfamiliar items. ''What's that stuff?''

''Diversionary paraphernalia,'' he replied briefly, withdrawing a large automatic pistol.

She gulped. ''Do you think you'll need that?''

''To talk the Falgettis into an exchange? Absolutely. The threat of a bullet between the eyes, unfortunately, is the only thing they understand.''

His words sent a shudder through her. ''What if they don't agree?''

''Then I go in alone.''

Katherine realized he meant what he said. She touched his arm, tears swimming in her eyes, knowing she couldn't ask for this supreme sacrifice despite the need to protect her child. "You don't have to do this."

His gaze met hers. "Yes, I do."

She swallowed, incredibly torn. She didn't want either of them to get hurt. "What do you want me to do?"

"As soon as Jessica and the boys step outside, pull the breakers," Paul instructed. "And no matter what else happens, run with Jessica and the boys."

"You mean if something happens to you?" she asked hoarsely.

He gripped her arms, their bodies closer than they'd been in weeks. "You have to trust me, Katherine—in spite of everything that's happened. It's our only chance."

She nodded. His eyes searched hers before he dropped his hands and eased away.

Trust. The one thing he'd broken. The one thing he now asked for. Did she have it in her? Somewhere so deep inside she'd refused to acknowledge it?

Holding that thought, she sprinted toward the house, slowing to cautious steps as she crept around the side. She carefully opened the cover to the breaker box, expecting a telltale creak, but it was silent.

Watching Paul, she saw him stop in the middle of the front yard. He tossed the rock he'd found at the front door.

The door opened slightly, the fallen rock illumi-

nated by the light that escaped. "Elliott?" a man
called, his deep voice harshly out of place in her
friend's home.

"It's me," Paul replied.

The door eased open a bit farther. "What's with
the rock?"

To Katherine's surprise, Paul chuckled as though
completely at ease. "It's new agency issue. Everybody knows the criminals have out-armed the
cops."

The man laughed, an ugly sound. "You alone,
Elliott?"

"That's what you wanted."

"That ain't no answer. You alone or not?"

"I didn't bring any agents or police," Paul replied, his stance still deceptively casual.

Despite her fear, Katherine watched in amazement. Paul seemed incredibly calm, as if he was
about to take a stroll down the beach, not look death
in the face.

"Why are you standing in the yard?" the man
asked suspiciously.

"It's safer that way."

The man's laugh was an abbreviated bark. "Not
from where I'm standing."

Paul's gun seemed to appear as though by magic,
aimed directly at the man, who started to move. "I
wouldn't do that," Paul warned. "You'd be dead
before you took a single step."

"I'm not alone here, you moron," the man replied. "Shoot me and my friend shoots the kid."

"I have a better idea," Paul suggested, as though discussing nothing more earth-shattering than the weather. "Bring the woman and kids to the front door. When they come outside, I walk in."

The man stared at the gun, apparently realizing Paul could drop him before he could run. "What's to keep you from shooting then?"

"As you just reminded me, your friend has a gun. I shoot you, he shoots me. Everybody loses. This way, the woman and kids get out. Then you and your friend face me."

Holding her breath, Katherine listened for the man's reply. He had a few muffled words with his partner, then grudgingly nodded and opened the door wider.

Heart lodged in her throat, she was just able to see Jessica holding the boys' hands as they crossed the threshold. When they reached the bottom of the steps, Katherine pulled the breakers, plunging the house into darkness.

"Run, Jess!" Paul yelled. "Run!"

Their feet clattered against the paved walkway just as several shots rang out. Paralyzed with fear, Katherine couldn't move at first. Had anyone been hit?

She bolted for the front yard in time to see Paul throw something into the house. Then she heard a soft boom just as Paul whipped a mask over his face and ran inside. More shots sounded from the house.

Katherine started toward Dustin when the noxious fumes reached her. Feeling dizzy, she paused.

Cars screeched to a halt in the street. The reinforcements, Katherine realized in a daze as men in flak jackets pulled on gas masks and rushed toward the house. As she watched, John leaped from one car and ran past her. Whirling around, she saw Jessica, the boys beside her.

She stumbled over to them as John pulled Jessica into his arms. Jessica seemed to resist for a moment before collapsing into his embrace.

Taking deep breaths to clear her head, Katherine hurried to Dustin and scooped him up into her arms. "Are you all right, baby?"

"Elly-ut saved us," Dustin told her, his sturdy little arms and legs locked around her.

"So he did, baby, so he did." The shooting had stopped inside, and the agents who'd remained outside were putting away their weapons. Still holding Dustin, Katherine looked toward the house to find Paul. At the same time, an ambulance arrived, siren blaring. "Thank God we don't need that," she told Dustin, smoothing back his hair.

But one of the agents was waving toward the paramedics, motioning for the gurney. Thinking one of the Falgettis must have been hit, she turned slightly, not wanting Dustin to see the man.

Then Paul staggered from the house, an agent on

either side of him, supporting him. As they started down the steps, Paul collapsed.

Katherine's pulse accelerated in fright. "Paul," she whispered.

"Elly-ut?" Dustin asked.

As she watched, the paramedics reached him with the gurney. Katherine rushed forward, but an agent put out his hand to stop her before she could get to his side. "Ma'am, we need to let the paramedics attend him."

Jessica, John and Brian joined them. Jessica took Dustin from Katherine while John spoke to the other agents.

Then he turned to Katherine. "You can ride in the ambulance with Paul."

Numbly she thanked him, pausing briefly to make certain Dustin felt safe in Jessica's arms. "We'll meet you at the hospital," Jessica assured her. "Dustin'll be fine."

The paramedics quickly loaded Paul into the ambulance and Katherine scrambled in behind them, her heart lodged in her throat. The wail of the siren split the night as the vehicle roared to life—accompanied by Katherine's desperately whispered prayers.

CHAPTER TWENTY-FOUR

THE WAITING ROOM hummed with voices and activity as doctors, nurses and technicians whisked by, their single-minded efficiency at once both frightening and comforting. The smell of coffee and antiseptic pushed away the remaining chemical fumes, but they weren't welcome distractions.

Katherine couldn't stop her torturous thoughts. What if Paul didn't make it? What if, in saving her son, he had sacrificed his own life?

Nurses had informed Katherine that the shot had ripped through Paul, damaging his liver and causing severe blood loss. He'd made it through the surgery, but was in critical condition. She wouldn't be able to see him for some time.

John and Jessica had arrived as soon as possible, having taken the children to her mother's house. Katherine had been grateful for their support. They hadn't allowed her to be alone until a few moments ago, when they had left to try to learn whether the doctors knew any more.

For the thousandth time, she marveled that Paul had been willing to risk his life for Dustin's. She had questioned what kind of man he was. Now she had proof that his character was the finest sort—this man she loved in a way she'd never loved before. But had fate conspired to snatch away both men she loved? Was this the second and cruelest blow?

Hearing footsteps, Katherine glanced up to see a doctor enter the waiting room.

"Mrs. Elliott?"

Terrified, she nodded, purposely not correcting his assumption that she was Paul's wife. She'd do whatever was necessary to obtain news about his condition.

"Your husband's stabilized," he began.

Katherine released breath she hadn't realized she was holding.

"But," the doctor warned, "he's still in critical condition."

Katherine couldn't prevent the tears blinding her. "Will he make it?" she managed in a choked voice.

Not completely unsympathetic, the doctor patted her hand. "The next few hours will tell."

SUNLIGHT CREPT through the blinds, weaving a pattern over the white cotton coverlet and metal bars of the hospital bed. Katherine leaned forward, watching Paul intently, as she had since the moment they'd brought him into the room.

He had passed the first crucial hours in intensive care. Just before dawn, they'd wheeled him into a private room in the critical-care unit. Katherine hadn't left his side since. The nurses frequently checked on him, and he was hooked up to an impressive monitoring system. But Katherine wanted to make certain that nothing was missed. She didn't have to worry about Dustin, knowing that Jessica would be especially tender with him after the traumatic incident.

Paul was so still, Katherine thought as she rose to stand next to the bed. So terribly still. Even when the nurses checked him, he didn't move. She had tamped down her own restlessness, her need to do something, anything, to help him. Instead, she waited and watched…and hoped and prayed.

But he hadn't moved. His eyelids remained closed.

What if she never had a chance to tell him how she felt? How important he was to her? Overcome with sadness, she closed her own eyes.

"Katherine?" Paul's weak whisper reached her.

At first she thought she'd imagined the sound. "Paul?" she asked shakily.

"It's me, funny face."

Unable to stem her tears, she turned away. Within moments she felt a tentative touch. Amazed, she looked down to see Paul's hand on her own. Lacing her fingers with his, Katherine lifted his hand to her mouth, kissing his fingers gently.

"I thought I'd lost you," she told him. "I was so scared."

"Wishful thinking," he teased weakly.

She gripped his hand. "Don't even joke about it.

I've been so stupid. I know now you did what you had to—because you loved Matthew. Before, I couldn't see past how this affected me. I never considered what it had done to you, how hurt you were. I shouldn't have—''

"Hey," he interrupted gently. "Does this mean you forgive me for impersonating Matthew?"

She nodded. "I think we're beyond that."

"I know I hurt you and I'm sorry I ever came up with such a lamebrain idea. All I ask is a chance to show you how much I love you."

Tears shimmered in her eyes. "How could you ever show me more than you already have? You gave me the life of my child." Katherine trembled, knowing she had so much more to tell him. "You gave me a kind of love I'd never known before." She met his eyes, wanting to be certain he understood. "And you made me love you in a way I didn't know was even possible." Her dark hair fell against his chest and draped over his arms as she bent close to him, her body shaking with sobs.

His fingers grasped a silky curl. "You're sure I'm still alive, funny face?"

She lifted her head, frightened that she'd caused a setback. "I'm sure. Do you need a nurse or a doctor? Or—"

"All I need is you, Katherine." His hand rested gently on her cheek. "Just you."

AWAY FROM THE BREAKING SURF of the rugged
shoreline, shell-topped roads wound through the
lush inland countryside. Sparsely populated, the land
was filled with tupelo trees and gloriously flowering
camellias. Honeysuckle vines wound mysteriously
around the trunks of saw palmetto trees, and Spanish
moss draped the wild arbor. The late-afternoon sun
poked through the leafy canopies, hinting at the
beauty of the approaching sunset. As the road
curved, it opened suddenly onto a long avenue of
ancient towering oaks.

The trees, planted centuries earlier by a young
man for his bride-to-be, created a passage as exqui-
site as the home they led to. Aged pink brick,
flanked by ivory pillars, soared upward with unas-
suming grace. It might have been a touch of
whimsy, but the chandelier seemed to sparkle in unprecedented fashion, as did the leaded windows
leading into the marble entryway. The house reeked
of romance, even mystery.

Rose Plantation. It was the house Katherine loved.

Sounds of laughter resounded gently off dusky-
pink walls. Sounds from people she loved.

Standing next to the wedding cake she'd designed
and created, Katherine met the eyes of her groom.
The man she loved.

For a moment she wondered if this was all a
dream. Paul stood so tall and straight. So very
strong. For weeks after the shooting, she had been
terrified, wondering if the bullet that had nicked his

spine had ended those days. But his determination to recover was as strong as the rest of him.

Katherine thought briefly of the past few weeks. It had been a time of harrowing discoveries, sadness and joy. They learned that Rod had fed the information to the Falgettis, which had allowed the criminals to place a temp at the reception.

To his dubious credit, Rod had ignorantly believed they were competitors, not killers, and he seemed genuinely horrified to learn what he'd been drawn into. He thought he was selling corporate secrets, not helping set up a murder. Paul had agreed that many people unknowingly involved themselves with the mob. Rod wasn't the first, but it was the most personal.

Jessica had been devastated to learn that her association with Rod, and her key to the building, had been used in such a terrible way. She had stumbled through apologies to both Katherine and Paul. Katherine assured her that nothing would ever destroy their precious friendship. Paul, in his strong quiet way, had been equally generous, enfolding Jessica in a hug and telling her that her friendship was the only key they cared about.

And John had helped the healing process. The night the Falgettis snatched Jessica and the children had been a wake-up call for all of them. To Katherine's delight, John had revealed his growing feelings for Jessica.

Now, looking at their maid of honor and best

man, dancing closely with eyes only for each other, Katherine believed Jessica and John's wedding would be next. It was better than the dream Jessica had wished for. This was reality, one that wouldn't vanish.

Katherine's gaze skipped over to her son, who was being watched by Jessica's mother. Dustin was dressed in a miniature tux exactly like Paul's for his role as ring bearer. Not wanting to exclude Brian, Paul had suggested they forgo the traditional flower girl. Instead, Brian, also dressed in a tux, had walked down the aisle with a second pillow. Each boy carried one of the rings. The small duo had charmed the guests.

"If you keep smiling, your face is going to freeze like that," Paul teased, slipping an arm around Katherine's waist.

Her smile widened. "That bad?"

"Damn near giddy," he replied, nuzzling her neck.

She shivered in anticipation as his breath warmed her bare shoulder. "I think I like giddy."

His lips trailed across her collarbone, pausing at the hollow of her throat. Her pulse gave an erratic leap. "Paul."

His eyes met hers. "I'm not Elliott to you anymore, am I?"

"I'm not sure you ever were. Some part of me knew almost from the start."

His gaze drifted over her upswept hair. She had

dispatched with the traditional headdress, opting to weave pearls through her hair, along with two flawless gardenias. A few defiant curls escaped. She was so damned beautiful it made him hurt. He knew it was time to give her his wedding gift.

He took her hands. "I tried to think of something to give you today, a gift that would let you know how much I cherish you. I searched, but there weren't any jewels to compete with the ones in your eyes." He paused. "And nothing could compare to the sweetness in your soul." Paul tightened his clasp on her hands. "And I couldn't wrap what I settled on."

"Which is?"

"A full-time husband and father." As her expression became faintly puzzled, he smiled. "I'm leaving the CIA. It's no life for a family man. It's not the kind of life I want to give you and Dustin."

Tears of joy shimmered in her eyes. "I have something special I was saving for you, too."

"You've already given me everything I could ever ask for," he replied.

"Maybe not quite everything," she told him, gratitude and love rolling through her. "I'm glad you want to be a full-time father, because our family's growing."

"Growing?" Realization dawned. "You mean…"

"Yes!" she cried. "And I'm almost certain it's a boy."

Their eyes met. Together they said the name. "Matthew."

Paul swallowed, the mix of emotions overpowering him. "It almost doesn't seem right that I'm so happy."

The ghosts of remembrance lingered between them. And Katherine smiled softly. "He'll be with us in our hearts always."

Their lips met in a gentle promise—a promise of joy, to be carried along into their forever.

If you enjoyed what you just read,
then we've got an offer you can't resist!

Take 2 bestselling love stories FREE!

Plus get a FREE surprise gift!

Clip this page and mail it to Silhouette Reader Service™

IN U.S.A.	**IN CANADA**
3010 Walden Ave.	P.O. Box 609
P.O. Box 1867	Fort Erie, Ontario
Buffalo, N.Y. 14240-1867	L2A 5X3

YES! Please send me 2 free Silhouette Romance® novels and my free surprise gift. Then send me 6 brand-new novels every month, which I will receive months before they're available in stores. In the U.S.A., bill me at the bargain price of $2.90 plus 25¢ delivery per book and applicable sales tax, if any*. In Canada, bill me at the bargain price of $3.25 plus 25¢ delivery per book and applicable taxes**. That's the complete price and a savings of over 10% off the cover prices—what a great deal! I understand that accepting the 2 free books and gift places me under no obligation ever to buy any books. I can always return a shipment and cancel at any time. Even if I never buy another book from Silhouette, the 2 free books and gift are mine to keep forever. So why not take us up on our invitation. You'll be glad you did!

215 SEN CNE7
315 SEN CNE9

Name _____ (PLEASE PRINT)

Address _____ Apt.# _____

City _____ State/Prov. _____ Zip/Postal Code _____

* Terms and prices subject to change without notice. Sales tax applicable in N.Y.
** Canadian residents will be charged applicable provincial taxes and GST.
   All orders subject to approval. Offer limited to one per household.
   ® are registered trademarks of Harlequin Enterprises Limited.

SROM99   ©1998 Harlequin Enterprises Limited

Return to the charm of the Regency era with

GEORGETTE HEYER,

creator of the modern Regency genre.

Enjoy six romantic collector's editions with forewords
by some of today's bestselling romance authors,

**Nora Roberts, Mary Jo Putney,
Jo Beverley, Mary Balogh,
Theresa Medeiros and Kasey Michaels.**

Frederica
On sale February 2000
The Nonesuch
On sale March 2000
The Convenient Marriage
On sale April 2000
Cousin Kate
On sale May 2000
The Talisman Ring
On sale June 2000
The Corinthian
On sale July 2000

Available at your favorite retail outlet.

HARLEQUIN®
Makes any time special ™

Visit us at www.romance.net   PHGHGEN

HARLEQUIN®
SUPERROMANCE®

**They look alike. They sound alike.
They act alike—at least some of the time.**

Two Sisters by **Kay David**
(Superromance #888)
A sister looks frantically for her missing twin.
And only a stranger can help her.
Available January 2000

The Wrong Brother by **Bonnie K. Winn**
(Superromance #898)
A man poses as his twin to fool the woman he thinks
is a murderer—a woman who also happens to be
his brother's wife.
Available February 2000

Baby, Baby by **Roz Denny Fox**
(Superromance #902)
Two men fight for the custody of twin babies.
And their guardian must choose who will be their father.
Available March 2000

Available wherever Harlequin books are sold.

HARLEQUIN®
Makes any time special ™

Visit us at www.romance.net

Come escape with Harlequin's new

Series Sampler

Four great full-length Harlequin novels bound together in one fabulous volume and at an unbelievable price.

Be transported back in time with a Harlequin Historical® novel, get caught up in a mystery with Intrigue®, be tempted by a hot, sizzling romance with Harlequin Temptation®, or just enjoy a down-home all-American read with American Romance®.

You won't be able to put this collection down!

On sale February 2000 at your favorite retail outlet.

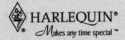

HARLEQUIN®
SUPERROMANCE®

Welcome to cowboy country!

MONTANA LEGACY by **Roxanne Rustand**
(Superromance #895)
Minneapolis cop Kate Rawlins has her own reasons
for wanting to sell her inheritance—half of the
Lone Tree Ranch, Montana. Then she meets
co-owner Seth Hayward and suddenly splitting the property
doesn't seem like a good idea....
On sale February 2000

COWBOY COME HOME by **Eve Gaddy**
(Superromance #903)
After years on the saddle circuit, champion bronco
rider Jake Rollins returns home—determined to find
out whether his ex-lover's daughter is *his* child.
On sale March 2000

Available at your favorite retail outlet.

HARLEQUIN®
Makes any time special ™